BLOOD AND TEARS

A DCI HARRY MCNEIL NOVEL

JOHN CARSON

DI FRANK MILLER SERIES

Crash Point
Silent Marker
Rain Town
Watch Me Bleed
Broken Wheels
Sudden Death
Under the Knife
Trial and Error
Warning Sign
Cut Throat
Blood from a Stone
Time of Death

Frank Miller Crime Series – Books 1-3 – Box set
Frank Miller Crime Series - Books 4-6 - Box set

MAX DOYLE SERIES

Final Steps
Code Red
The October Project

SCOTT MARSHALL SERIES

Old Habits

BLOOD AND TEARS

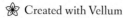 Created with Vellum

For the real Eve Bell

ONE

They had never met each other before. They didn't move in the same social circles. They didn't live in the same part of the city. But they did have one thing in common.

They were both seasoned killers.

Dr Kenneth Conrad and Archie Higgins had been caught, jailed and transported to Edinburgh's High Court for sentencing. On the same day. Which was nothing unusual in itself, it just gave the press a field day.

'Get a move on!' one of the court officers shouted at them as they entered the transport area of the High Court building. It was on the lower level of the building on the high street, with its entrance onto St Giles Street.

The large van was waiting for them, like some removal van for human beings, although they weren't being treated like human beings at the moment.

One of the court officers pushed Conrad and he turned to look at the man.

'Got a problem?' the officer said to him. 'No? I didn't think so. I'm not old enough for you to murder, am I?'

Conrad's position of being innocent until proven guilty was long gone and now he was looking at spending the rest of his life in prison.

'Sit in the back of the van and behave yourself or else those boys will not be quite so lenient as we are.' He nodded to the security team who were dealing with the transfer back to Barlinnie.

Conrad didn't say a word but turned round when he heard the door being opened again and Archie Higgins was brought through. The court officer who escorted him waited for the security team from the prisoner transport service to take over.

Conrad had begun to look away when the first explosion happened.

Flames shot out of the gaps around the front of the van.

'What the hell was that?' one of the court officers shouted as the driver jumped out.

'The engine's on fire!' the driver shouted.

Another explosion and smoke billowed heavily from the front of the van, quickly filling the vehicle bay. It wasn't a large area, just big enough to hold one van at a time.

Conrad felt panic well up inside.

'Get them back upstairs!' the officer yelled but as he tried to open the door leading back to the court, he found it locked.

There was a security office on one side, which was

supposed to be manned at all times, but the guard could see it was empty. Where the hell was his colleague? He couldn't see anybody, but there was chaos, with men shouting and the smoke getting thicker. The flames were becoming more intense.

The guard ran into the office, coughing profusely as he went, and tripped over the officer who was in charge of the door. Panic shot through him, as he thought that maybe the other man had had a heart attack. He hit the fire alarm button and the siren started wailing.

They were trapped in here and he realised there was no choice but to open the roller door. He knew if he tried to resuscitate the prone guard, he would die.

The smoke was like nothing he had ever seen, getting thicker and thicker. 'Get those two men back in handcuffs!' he shouted. There was no answer. He brought a hanky out and covered his mouth as he exited the small office. As he rushed out, daylight started streaming into the loading bay.

Protocol was to have any prisoner handcuffed to a security officer before the door was opened in such an emergency as this, and he expected his colleagues to have known this. Maybe not the new crowd, he thought, hoping that they had paid attention at the training courses. The new security company had been given the contract to escort prisoners to and from the prisons, and the officer hoped to hell they were on the ball.

Then his foot caught something. Or *somebody*. His other colleague was sprawled on the floor. He coughed and ducked, trying to stay low. What was going on? Yet, he knew in his heart what was going on.

Too late, he saw the man in the gas mask appear in front of him, and then something hit him over the head and he went down hard.

Kenneth Conrad expected a hand to fall on his shoulder at any moment, but nothing came. There were shouts amid the confusion. The smoke was belching like an old steam train. More explosions came from the front of the van. Flames had grabbed a hold of the vehicle and were having a good time with it, eating away at its very fibre.

Conrad stood coughing and watched as the masked men pushed the van slowly forward, out through the open doorway and into the street, the flames rapidly expanding. More smoke now as the air caught the fire.

There was movement. Shouting; voices issuing orders from behind gas masks.

Where was Higgins?

Then Conrad saw him. Christ, this was no accident. The stairway door was well alight now as one of the men wearing a gas mask splashed petrol on it. The fire alarms assaulted his ears. The guards who had brought them through from Glasgow were taking their uniforms off and slipping into civilian clothes. They were all wearing gas masks.

Then a hand grabbed his arm.

The man lifted his gas mask and Conrad looked into the face of Archie Higgins.

'Don't let the bastards beat you, Kenny, old son. Get your arse out into the sunshine.'

Higgins led him towards the door, and now they were both coughing. The smoke was stinging Conrad's eyes.

'There you go, pal,' Higgins said as they approached the back door. 'Freedom.'

Conrad watched as other men in the security company's uniform opened what seemed like a hundred smoke grenades. The fire in the front of the van was getting more intense by the second, and then something else exploded from the front of it. The whole cab was gone now.

There were shouts and screams from outside and Conrad could see more vehicles on fire in the street.

Conrad hesitated for a moment. 'There's people out there,' he said.

Higgins called one of the guards over. 'Give Kenny some money.'

'Sure, boss.' The man's voice was muffled behind his gas mask. He reached into a pocket and thrust a thick wad of notes into Conrad's hand. Twenties and tens.

'Thanks.' The fresh air felt good but the smoke was pouring out of the entrance.

'We only have about three minutes. You can stay or go, it's your choice, pal.' Higgins coughed and pulled his mask off the rest of the way and tossed it aside. A couple of the men released even more smoke grenades and threw them around.

Conrad only hesitated for a few more seconds before he walked out into the street.

It was chaos outside, with the fire inside the loading bay now gaining more traction.

Conrad started striding along St Giles Street, not daring to look back. He was wearing a shirt and tie and his best suit. He wouldn't stand out amongst all the lawyers and court staff around here. The place was always hooching with suits.

There was the sudden sound of motorbikes revving and he realised how Higgins was going to get away from there.

Conrad reached the entrance to the News Steps and quickly turned around, expecting to see a dozen police uniforms descending on him, but all he saw was the smoke billowing out of the receiving bay, the van in the middle of the street on fire and a few journalists and photographers, dancing about like they were the ones who were on fire. Conrad wished they were.

He looked for the uniforms but there were none. Only a small group of businessmen getting into a minibus with blacked-out windows and driving away from the burning van, slipping into traffic and blending with all the other moving metal.

There was no sign of Higgins or... who? The guards who had helped him escape? That was surely what happened, but he went down the stone steps at a clip that would see him get down speedily without either falling and breaking his neck, or arousing suspicion that he was a handbag snatcher.

When he reached Market Street below, a police car came firing towards him from the direction of Waverley

Station, and he thought his taste of freedom had been short but very sweet. Now it was time to sit in the back of a police car again.

The patrol car shot past him.

Conrad smiled, his heart beating fast, and he carried on walking down the hill, crossing over Cockburn Street and heading to the back entrance of Waverley Station.

Sirens split the air. He looked and saw fire engines turn from Waverley Bridge onto Market Street, going up the hill the way the police car had. Smoke was rising into the clear afternoon sky.

Conrad turned and strolled down the steps into the station.

And melted into the crowd.

TWO

Detective Sergeant Robbie Evans dropped into the driver's seat of the pool car, with a bacon roll and a cup of coffee.

'The bloody car's honking already,' Detective Chief Inspector Jimmy Dunbar said from the passenger seat.

'It's just bacon. Don't tell me you've gone off bacon rolls now?' He unwrapped it and took a bite and a bit of ketchup squeezed out of the side and touched his cheek.

'Messy bastard. Don't be getting that pish on me.'

'You don't know what you're missing,' Evans replied after washing the bit of roll down with some coffee from the polystyrene cup.

'That's the point, I *do* know what I'm missing; bloody sauce dripping down my tie. Hardened arteries. High blood pressure. That's what the doc told me and I'm listening this time. No more cakes or crap.'

'You're a lot older than me so it stands to reason an old codger would have to watch what he eats.'

'Cheeky bastard. You'll be an old codger one day, pal.'

Evans finished his roll and then his coffee. 'Nah. If I ever found out that I was going to be dumped on the scrap heap, I would go out in a blaze of glory. I can't stand the thought of not being able to do what I want, when I want to do it. Then have somebody wipe my arse for me.' He turned to look at Dunbar.

'What are you fucking looking at me for? And that's good to know, that you want to go out in a ball of flames. This will be the last time you're driving us about. When it's my time to go, I want it to be in the company of my wife, in a wee country hotel after spending an exciting few days. No burning, no blazes, just slipping away with a grin on my face.'

'I don't mean I want to go out now, obviously. I've still got a lot of life left in me.'

'Not if you keep eating shite like that bacon roll.'

Evans grinned. 'I do like your idea better, I have to admit. Spending a weekend with a girl then popping my clogs just before we check out. That would save paying the bill, too.'

'Suicidal, tight-wad and manky bastard all rolled into one. You've got it all going for you, eh? Just fucking drive. And if I see you going one mile per hour over the speed limit, I'll boot you in the bollocks as soon as look at you.'

Evans grinned again as he wiped his face and started the car.

'What did Cathy make for your lunch?' He nodded

to the lunch box that sat unopened in the footwell as he pulled into traffic.

'Never you bloody mind what she made me.'

'I bet it has lettuce, your wee box.'

'I'll shove it up *your* wee box. And the salad has some chicken in it, if you must know.'

'Jeez, Jimmy, we won't recognise you if you lose weight. They'll be saying, *Who said that?* in the incident room, you'll be that thin.'

'Am I going to hear this every fucking day, just because I'm on a health kick?'

'Maybe I should try a decent diet?'

'Why? You've eaten nothing but shite since I've known you. Why change now? Fat bastard.'

'Well, I wasn't going to say anything, but...' He stopped for a red light.

'What? Your mother's clothes don't fit you anymore and you have to go up one size? Never mind, son, there are lots of nice dresses in Oxfam.'

'You would know.'

'I *would* know. My Cathy shops there for shirts and stuff. While I look at books.'

'But anyway. As I was going to say, I have something to tell you.'

'Christ, you really do wear your mother's fucking dresses. What's that called again? Cross dressing or something. You got a pair of her skids on now? Manky bastard.'

'Gie yersel' peace. Bloody skids. No, Jimmy, I found a new girlfriend.'

'Where about? Buried in the woods, wrapped in plastic?'

'You know, if this DCI gig ever gets old for you, then maybe you could do stand-up for a living. You'd make hee haw, though, 'cause your jokes are pish.' He drove off at the green light.

'Don't start greetin' now. Tell Uncle Jimmy about this new *girlfriend*.' He used finger quotes.

'I met her online.'

'Oh aye? Where? *Ladyboys R Us?*'

'You know what, I'm telling you sod all from now on.'

'Okay, okay, tell me.'

'We were pen pals. I want to go to America but I wanted to chat to a woman first, so I met her, and now we've become an item.'

'An item? Like Posh and Becks? More like Pished on Becks, knowing you.'

'Put your green face away, *Uncle* Jimmy. She's gorgeous, wants to come across to Scotland and loves the idea of coming over to Glasgow. Then I can fly back with her to America.'

Dunbar looked sceptical. 'Where does she live ?'

'Boston.'

'Have you spoken to her on the phone?'

'Of course I have. And we Skype.'

'And she's not under supervision, being watched over by a man in a white coat?'

'Of course not. She's a looker. Here, let me get my phone out and I'll show you a photo.'

'Keep your fucking hands on the wheel. This is not

the day you're going to go out in a fireball. Not with me in the bloody passenger seat. I've no doubt one day you'll crash and burn, but not this afternoon. Old squeaky baws wants to see us.'

Detective Superintendent Calvin Stewart, Dunbar's boss.

'What does he want?'

'Maybe he wants my salad. He can have the fucking thing. The smell of that bacon roll is making me hungry.' Dunbar looked at him. 'If you ever eat a roll in front of me again, I'll shove my piece box up your jacksie.'

They parked round the back of the Helen Street police station in Govan and went in the back door, heading straight to Stewart's office upstairs.

'Come!' Stewart shouted and Dunbar entered the office, Evans following closely behind.

'Don't bother sitting,' the older man said. He always had red cheeks as if he sat in his office all day slapping himself.

'You two are both going through to work in Edinburgh again. I was just on the phone with the chief constable, and he wants you working for his ex-missus, Jeni Bridge. You're going to fill them in, Dunbar.'

'Fill them in on what, sir?'

'Haven't you heard? That fucking bawbag Archie Higgins just escaped from custody. And guess what?'

Dunbar stood and waited. 'Enlighten us, sir,' he said, after it was apparent that Stewart really did want them to guess.

'Kenneth Conrad fucked off as well.'

'Conrad?' Dunbar said. The doctor who did for the National Health Service reputation what Jack the Ripper did for the London Tourist Board.

'The very same. Apparently, he was in the same fucking prison van as Higgins. They set fire to it and the court loading bay. Now some of the guards have fucked off with them. It's a real mess, Jimmy. Go and sort it out. And take what's-his-face there with you. Pack a suitcase. Arrangements are being made for you to stay in that hotel again. I hope we get a bloody discount.'

'*What's-his-face?*' Evans said in the corridor outside as they walked away. 'I'll rip him a new arsehole.'

Stewart's office door opened and he poked his head out.

'Go on then,' Dunbar said in a low voice, grinning.

'One thing; can you take your own car, Evans? We're tight on pool cars right now.'

'Yes, sir.'

Stewart disappeared back into his office and the door closed.

'Well that fucking told him,' Dunbar said.

'Aye, well, he caught me off balance.'

Dunbar shook his head. 'Just go and get the intel we have on Higgins and Conrad, then we can go through to Edinburgh in that fucking death trap you call a car. I want to be the one to nail the bastards.'

THREE

Angie Patterson, one of the mortuary assistants, let DCI Harry McNeil and DS Alex Maxwell into the city mortuary via the door next to the loading bay roller door.

'Hi, Harry,' she said. 'Alex.'

'Hi, Angie.' The smell of the place hit Harry's nostrils but he'd skipped lunch in preparation of this afternoon's festival of fun.

She smiled at them. 'Have you two set the date yet?'

'I want to officially propose first,' Harry said, and the words sounded lame even to him.

'Well, I'm over the moon for you both.' She looked at his closely-shaved head. 'That wee scar is healing well. I hope having your noggin' bashed in didn't affect your judgement?'

'What do you mean?' Harry said.

'I mean, that lassie won't wait around forever. And you call yourself a detective?'

'We've had a lot on our plate. Alex got injured too, and her recuperation took a wee while longer than mine.'

Angie turned round. Put a hand on her hair. 'Do you see the zipper on the back of my head?' She turned round to face them again. 'I thought not.'

'If I'd known I was going to be having so much fun, I'd have called round sooner.'

'Next time I'll bake a cake. Come on, the reception committee's waiting upstairs.'

'Leo Chester here?' Alex asked.

'No, the great professor is off on holiday. It's Kate Murphy and the almighty Doctor Dagger.'

They rode up in the lift until they got to the PM suite.

'Hello, detectives,' Kate said, smiling at them as they put the coveralls on.

'Hi, Kate,' Alex said.

Harry waved. His stomach was doing flips. Post-mortem exams always had this effect on him, but he was determined not to give in to it. That was something he hadn't missed when he had worked in Professional Standards. The smell, watching somebody's lifeless corpse being turned inside out. One day, he'd thought he could hear a wailing from outside in the corridor, the wailing of an anguished soul who was watching herself being dissected, some old woman who was full of maggots and yellow liquid—

'Harry!' Kate said.

He shook his head and tried moving his tongue in the little desert he called his mouth.

'Sorry. Miles away.'

Alex had grabbed a little paper cup and filled it with water from the dispenser behind the door. He took it from her, drained the contents, and noticed the two doctors were watching him like he was the star.

He scrunched it up, threw it towards a bin and missed. 'Fuck,' he said under his breath, but left it there.

'Right, let's get this show on the road,' Dagger said.

He inserted the knife into the man's chest, making the classic Y-shape, then he peeled the skin and flesh back.

It's only a dummy. We're on the set of a horror film and this is just a film we're making. We're all actors and the camera crew is behind me, out of sight. Any minute now, the director will shout Cut! *And this will be over. The corpse will sit up and smile and then we'll all go home.*

Nobody shouted *Cut!* and no second-unit director told them what a good job they were doing, to go home, and they'd see them tomorrow.

This corpse was real. He had been stabbed to death after he got into a fight after stepping off a bus. Harry could see the defence wounds on the man's hands and arms. He had fought valiantly and although he couldn't talk to them now, the pathologist would help tell his story.

'The tip of the knife cut his femoral artery in his groin,' Kate said. Harry nodded, trying to unsee the man's organs that had just been removed. It was a wonder he wasn't a vegetarian by now, but later that night, maybe he'd have a salad for dinner. No meat, just the green bits with some dressing. Hopefully there would be no maggots crawling about unseen in it.

'Definitely homicide,' Kate said. 'Cause of death is bleeding from a cut artery. Poor sod. He had a heart attack and a stroke after the artery was cut and his organs were being starved of blood.'

'Thanks, Kate,' Harry said. *Are you trying to make me puke?*

Big, bad Harry McNeil had never got to grips with going to the post-mortems of victims. The smell, the sight of their insides being put on display. The buzz saw cutting through bone.

He had never been affected by seeing a corpse in situ, but it was the chemical smell of the mortuary that got him. The noise of the tools and watching the handling of the organs like they were pieces of cow in a butcher's window.

They left the post-mortem suite, ditching the coveralls into a large basket, the gloves and overshoes into the bin.

'You looked like you wanted to be anywhere but there,' Alex said. 'My big, brave boy.'

'You're so funny.' His phone vibrated in his pocket. The sound was off. He listened to the caller on the other end before hanging up.

'We have to go, sharpish,' he said. 'The prisoner, Archie Higgins? Getting sentenced today?'

Alex nodded.

'He's not a prisoner anymore.'

FOUR

Harry and Alex were tasked with picking up Dunbar and Evans so they took a pool car to the hotel in Stockbridge, round the corner from where they lived.

'Hey, Harry, Alex. Good to see you again.'

'Hi, Jimmy. Where's young Robbie?'

They were in the small beer garden in front of the hotel, waiting on the DS. Dunbar looked at his watch. 'The bloody toe rag better shift his arse.' He shook his head. 'He's in love.'

'Got himself a girlfriend then?' Alex said, when they saw Evans coming out the front door of the hotel.

'Aye, he met her on one of those sex sites. Some old boiler puts up a photo of a supermodel and young studs like Robbie here drool over her.'

Evans ignored him as he looked at the screen of his phone. 'I'm not sure what time we'll be done, but I'll call you.'

He looked at the other three officers. 'What? I was just telling her I'd be late talking to her.'

'She's a nice lassie,' Dunbar said. 'She's going to teach him how to play the banjo.'

'You know what, it must be sad, getting to your age and being jealous of a younger colleague.'

'Yeah, that's what it is, son. Nothing to do with experience or anything like that. Now, if you can put your bloody phone away for five minutes, maybe we can get up to the High Street.'

Evans put his phone away. Dunbar stood looking at him.

'What?' Evans said.

'The file? The info we have on Higgins and Conrad?'

'I remembered. I just wanted to come down and say hello to our friends first.'

'For God's sake, Robbie, get a move on.'

Evans turned and sprinted back into the hotel, returning a few minutes later.

'All you had to do was ask,' he said.

'It must be love,' Harry said.

They got into the pool car and Alex drove through Stockbridge up to the High Street.

The conference room in the station was full of senior officers and there was a buzz of noise as they entered the packed room.

Jeni Bridge, commander of Police Scotland, Edinburgh Division, looked up from the end of the table. She was sitting next to Detective Chief Superintendent Percy Purcell. She stood up.

'Ladies and gentlemen, can we all be seated, please.'

The noise filtered down to zero as they all sat.

Jeni looked around the room, then at Dunbar. 'For those of you who are not familiar with them, we have DCI Jimmy Dunbar and his colleague, DS Robbie Evans, through from Glasgow. Thank you for coming at short notice.'

Dunbar smiled. Considering the chief constable was Jeni Bridge's ex-husband, when he said get over to Edinburgh to work on the case with Commander Bridge, there was no arguing.

'As we all know, a manhunt was launched two and a half hours ago after two prisoners escaped from the secure holding area over the road at the High Court. The reason DCI Dunbar is here is because both prisoners are from Glasgow and had just been handed life sentences for murder. He was the arresting officer in the Dr Kenneth Conrad case and had worked on the Archie Higgins case. DCI Dunbar, we would appreciate a rundown from you, even though we have the files. Sometimes it's better from the horse's mouth, as it were.'

'Certainly.' Dunbar stood up and addressed the room. 'Let me start with Archie Higgins. I'll let you read up on his age and height and all the boring stuff, but allow me to give you a rundown on the man himself, things that the papers didn't get to print.' He looked at some of the faces, like a magician on stage might do to spot any disbeliever.

'I've known him for years. A real Janus; he can be the perfect guest at any social gathering; witty, charming, full of anecdotes. He can also be your worst nightmare. And yes, I know that sounds clichéd, but if ever it applied to anybody, it's this man. He's a real hard man, a gangster in every sense of the word. But we could never pin anything on him. Not one single thing. He surrounds himself with men who are above loyal. They will do anything for him, they are well rewarded, and Higgins never gets his hands dirty.

'Except one time. And that proved to be his downfall. It started with somebody killing one of his wee girls. Sixteen-year-old Rebecca...'

FIVE

Two years earlier

'Becca, Christine, c'mon, for fuck's sake. We're going to be late.' Archie Higgins stood in their large kitchen in the new house in Bearsden, alternating between looking at his watch and taking a swig of the whisky from the crystal glass.

'Archie, for God's sake, do you have to use language like that in front of the lassie?' his wife, Candy, said.

Archie looked at her. 'I didn't say it loud enough for her to hear me from all the way upstairs. Besides, we are going to be late.' He smiled at his wife. Candy Red. That was what his nickname for her had been. He had fallen in love with her the moment he saw her. She was beautiful, with bright green eyes, auburn hair, and a killer smile.

Archie knew he wanted to see more of her. He had never in his life felt that way about a woman. They had stayed up all night to talk. About everything under the sun. Just talk, no more. He felt happy with that.

And so began a relationship that had continued into marriage and two beautiful little girls, Rebecca and Christine. Rebecca had just turned sweet sixteen and was going to be the star of the show. Her birthday party. It was going to be a night they would remember for the rest of their lives. Everyone for a different reason.

The party was held in an upmarket hotel in Glasgow city centre. Archie wanted something special for his little girl. A five-star hotel it was. With a big ballroom filled with friends and family. One of whom was going to change the course of the lives of the main players.

His name was Benedict St Charles. Archie assumed the name had to be made up, but Becca told him the man was her friend's uncle.

The alcohol was for adults only. Archie had some of his staff members there to enforce this rule and it worked. The kids had a great time and so did the adults. Only St Charles was showing signs of becoming a pest. He was a tall, skinny man, balding on top. He was nothing to look at but that didn't stop him clowning around on the dance floor with the women; another man, who seemed to be his wingman, egging him on.

'Who's he?' Archie said to one of his men, Eddie Wise.

Eddie was head of Archie's security and he indicated for one of the underlings to come over with the clipboard. The names and sign-in times were written on the paper.

'Who's that joker on the dance floor?' Archie asked.

23

'Name's Benedict St Charles. His brother's name is Ralf. He made a song and dance about me pronouncing his name wrong. It's *Raif*, he said. They're the uncles of one of the guests.'

Archie made a face. 'Fucking Raif. Keep an eye on him. First sign he's going to be trouble, assure him he's at the wrong fucking do.'

'Will do, sir.' He walked away leaving the security chief with the boss.

'I don't like that bastard, Eddie. In fact, he's getting too close to my daughter for my liking. When this song ends, tell the DJ to give it a rest for a minute, then empty that St Charles twat out the door.'

'Which one?'

'I have a feeling that when one of them is getting the heave-ho, the other one won't be far behind. Make it happen, Eddie.'

'Right on it, sir.'

The dance floor was packed but the St Charles brothers were nowhere to be seen.

Archie wasn't too concerned at first, and put the order out to keep an eye on them, but nobody could see them. They hadn't come with any women, and when discreet enquiries were made, it turned out that Benedict had brought his brother along as his plus one. Neither men were married as far as anybody knew.

Archie wasn't worried until he couldn't see his daughters anymore.

'Eddie, where's Becca and Chrissie?' he asked his security man.

'I didn't see them, boss.'

'Get one of the girls to go and check the toilets. Discreetly.'

Eddie nodded and a few minutes later, came back shaking his head. 'They're not there.'

Archie felt the panic kick in. He walked over to where Candy was standing talking to some of her friends from the PTSA. He gently grabbed her elbow, not wanting to alarm her, and guided her away.

'Where's the girls?' he said, his voice hushed.

Candy's face changed in an instant. 'What do you mean? They're on the dance floor.' She looked over to where people were dancing, having a laugh.

'No, they're not. Didn't you see them go anywhere?'

Candy looked back at him. 'Becca was over there a few minutes ago. Are you sure she's not there?'

'Of course I'm sure. I've Eddie and the boys looking for them but we can't find them.'

'Maybe Becca went up to the room to get changed out of her ball gown.'

Archie looked at his watch. 'She was going to do that later, before we went home. It's way too early for that.'

'I'll go up there with Eddie. If she has decided to change early, then I don't want her embarrassed with your men rushing in.'

Archie clicked his fingers and Eddie appeared at his side.

'Take Candy up to the room to see if Becca's there. Take some of the team with you. I'll stay here in case she comes back. If you do see her, don't panic her. Get somebody to eyeball Chrissie.'

Candy left with some of her husband's men, heading upstairs to one of the rooms they'd booked to change in. Archie was looking around, the music loud, then suddenly one of his men was at his side, a heavy hand on his arm.

Archie could see the panic on the man's flushed face. No words were needed.

They turned and ran out of the ballroom, heading up the stairs. He could hear the yells coming from the room. His people were outside, and he could hear shouts and screams.

He pushed past the suits and saw his wife sitting on the bed, cradling their daughter, whose party dress was ripped. There was blood on Rebecca's face as if she'd been punched. Her hair was ruffled and blood was spattered across her dress.

Chrissie was on the bathroom floor, her knees up to her chin. Higgins got down on his knees and held her in his arms.

It was the limpness that got Archie. Seeing his daughters like rag dolls.

He could hear the shouts from somebody saying an ambulance was on its way, another voice telling people to get out of the room. He thought it was Eddie but couldn't be sure. He couldn't see clearly. His hearing was muffled, like his brain was trying to shut down. Maybe it was the blood rushing through his head, he couldn't be sure. He sat on the floor, cradling his daughter, looking over to his wife and older daughter. He wanted to move but his legs wouldn't work.

Then the paramedics rushed in after what seemed like hours. They said she was still alive, but it looked like she had a head injury. The room was cleared of unnecessary people. Archie knew what would happen now; the police would turn up and trample over everything.

He started crying then and his legs went weak but Eddie held onto him and for the first time in his life, Archie Higgins let his emotions show in public.

Then he took a deep breath and stepped back from his friend. 'I want that bastard, Eddie. Find out who he is, and where he lives. Money no object. Do it now, before the police get here.'

He watched as Rebecca was taken out on a stretcher and Christine was led away by her mother.

SIX

A pin could be heard dropping as Jimmy Dunbar stopped and looked around the room.

'What happened next?' Jeni Bridge asked.

'This is what the prosecution theorised because Archie Higgins wasn't caught with his hand in the biscuit tin, as it were. On that night, we were called to the hotel. Rebecca Higgins had been taken to the hospital, where she died six hours later. Head trauma. Christine was still alive but in shock. Becca had been attacked and we surmised they got disturbed before young Christine could be assaulted. Archie's wife was a wreck, but she managed to tell the lead officer who had been dancing with Becca and her friends, and he was soon identified.'

'I'm assuming they didn't hang around?' Percy Purcell said.

'Correct, sir. Both St Charles brothers were nowhere to be found, but we quickly got an address for Benedict, though by the time we got to his flat, he had been murdered. Stabbed to death. There was blood everywhere, but there was no sign of Ralf. He's never been seen since. We think one was murdered while the other was taken away for a real going over. When forensics dusted the place, Archie Higgins' fingerprints were found at the scene. When he was picked up, he denied killing St Charles, and claimed he had never been to his flat. When the team confronted him with the fact his fingerprints were at the scene, he changed his story. He said he did indeed go round there that night, but St Charles was already dead and there was no sign of his brother. He wouldn't tell us where Ralf was.'

'And this Ralf was never found?'

'No. He vanished off the face of the earth. All known addresses were checked and nobody had seen him. We think he was taken somewhere and killed.'

'And Higgins was convicted by a jury,' Jeni said.

'He was indeed, ma'am. He was in court today for formal sentencing after psychiatric tests were ordered by his defence team, but that argument was thrown out. A jury found him guilty and he was sentenced to life.'

'And now he's running free,' Purcell said. 'Along with *Doctor Death*, as the press call Kenneth Conrad.'

'Any questions?' Jeni said.

'Was there any connection between Conrad and Higgins before they were in Barlinnie?' Harry asked.

'As far as we're aware, there was no connection before today. They rode in the security van together. I've asked for reports to be sent through from the Big Hoose, and they should be with you shortly, ma'am.' He nodded to Jeni again.

The Big Hoose was a slang name for Barlinnie.

'What can you tell us about Conrad?' Purcell asked. The information had quickly been collated into a brief report but there was nothing like it coming from the horse's mouth.

'Doctor Kenneth Conrad is a very unassuming man. You wouldn't look twice at him in the street. Which is the way for a lot of killers. He might have got away with his crimes if it wasn't for one stupid mistake he made...'

SEVEN

The old woman's bedroom window overlooked Bearsden Golf Club.

'My father always wanted a hole-in-one at the club, but all he got was a drinking problem and an empty wallet,' the daughter said as she stood looking out at the greens. She turned to look at Dr Kenneth Conrad as he stuffed his paraphernalia into his bag. She looked tired, the bags under her eyes belonging to a woman ten years older.

'Your mother's needing some rest now,' Conrad said. 'We can talk downstairs.'

The daughter, Edwina Adams, looked almost relieved, as if she had been craving conversation; her mother was incapable. The drugs didn't make for a chatty companion.

They went down to the large living room. Conrad stood in the middle of the room as if waiting for directions. *Conrad enters stage left and sits on the settee while the daughter hovers awkwardly, waiting to offer a nice cup of tea.*

'Sit down in your chair, doctor. Can I get you a nice cup of tea?'

His chair. 'That would be acceptable,' he said, putting his bag down on the floor next to a chair with doilies on the arms. Crocheted by somebody who was born in another time. He half expected the daughter to ask him not to put his arms on them, but wasn't that the point? She said nothing, merely buzzing out of the living room with renewed vigour, now that she had a newfound purpose, other than to watch her mother die.

Conrad tapped his fingers on the chair. This was his last and only house call of the day. Mrs Davina Adams didn't have much more time on this earth so she couldn't make it into the surgery anymore. Hospice staff were coming in daily, to support the work her daughter was doing, but he, as her GP, came in every day now, just to make sure things were going as smoothly as possible; as much as dying could go smoothly.

'I put an extra digestive on your plate,' Edwina Adams said as she came into the room. *Davina and Edwina.* He'd tried saying it fast three times but always tripped himself up.

He took the cup on the saucer with a smile, and kept his eye on the tea as he accepted the plate of digestives. He felt like a circus act about to set the china on fire and start juggling. He managed to set the cup down on the side table without spilling anything on the shag pile.

Since he'd been coming here every day for the past

two weeks, this had become *his chair*. Maybe Edwina would get him a pair of slippers next. A nice pipe to go with it. Adopt a cat from the animal shelter so it could lay on the back of *his chair*.

He sipped the tea. It was just as he liked it, a little on the strong side. Edwina had perfected it on his third visit. And while he hadn't exactly complained about the rich tea biscuits, he had hinted that maybe a chocolate Hobnob wouldn't go amiss, but she was obviously working her way up to those. The digestives were the biscuit equivalent of a halfway house. *Be a good boy and you'll get your Hobnobs.*

Except he wasn't going to be around long enough to graduate to those particular treats.

'Davina really needs to go into the hospice now, Edwina.' He said it in a gentle voice, dunking his digestive quickly into the tea before pulling it back out, unlike the first time he'd tried it and it had got too soggy too quickly and had gone rogue on him and fallen into the brown liquid. If Edwina had noticed, she hadn't mentioned it.

'Don't say that, Kenneth.' Edwina brought a paper hanky out of her sleeve like a magician and held it up to her face as she started to cry. Then she balled it up and fired it into a small bin by the side of the settee.

He took a clean handkerchief out of his pocket and gave it to her. 'Dab your eyes with that,' he said, and watched as it made its way to her nose. It was one of his monogrammed ones. *Note to self; bring one from the Marks and Sparks pack tomorrow.*

'It's not fair on Davina, but more to the point, it's not fair on *you*.'

She dabbed her eyes with a dry piece and tucked it up her sleeve like the paper one had never existed. 'Michael didn't see it that way.'

She used a recriminating tone before looking at him. Michael Salamin, another doctor in the practice. A locum, covering for somebody being off long-term. Conrad had brought him along a few times to meet the old lady. To get to know her, should he be called out when he, Conrad wasn't available. Plus, being the locum, more often than not, he was put on the overnight on-call roster.

Conrad didn't feel guilty. The man had to learn the ropes. After all, in a month's time, Conrad would be away, taking an extended holiday, and Salamin wouldn't be the new kid on the block anymore, as yet another new recruit would step up.

'Michael's new. He hasn't known you as long as I have. I know what's best for Davina. But more importantly, I know what's best for you. You're running yourself into the ground, Edwina. And with the best will in the world, you're burning yourself out.' Another quick dunk into the tea then the first digestive was gone. 'I mean, when was the last time you had a holiday? Like a trip to Blackpool or something?'

She took a deep breath and let it out before lifting her own cup. She took a sip and the room was so quiet, the clink of the cup going back onto the saucer sounded like a rifle shot.

'I wouldn't go to Blackpool. There's too much...' She looked at the ceiling for a moment.

Drink? Sex? Rock 'n' Roll? Conrad took his second biscuit, about to give it a good dunking when Edwina looked over at him.

'Noise. All that racket. Trams clanging about day and night. Youngsters shouting and getting drunk. No, I wouldn't like that. Mother and I went to Berwick one time. We stayed in a static caravan.'

Hardly gunfight at the OK caravan park though, was it? 'Maybe you need a little bit of relaxation though, Edwina. Maybe go on holiday with some friends.'

She laughed but it came out as a snort of derision. 'Friends? I don't call them friends anymore, the ones I used to go out with. Even my friends at the rural are more my mother's age.'

Conrad didn't know what the rural was exactly, some sort of knitting club, where he suspected women of an age greater than Edwina's gathered to exchange patterns and gossip. Not exactly jumping with eligible bachelors.

'There must be somebody you could go out with. Maybe your sister.'

'Karina has her own life. She has kids. A job she didn't have to leave in order to look after our mother. She's not interested in going out with me on a Friday night. Besides, who would look after mother?'

'The hospice would provide a nurse for you while you went out for a little while. You need a break.'

'I'll get a break when mother's... not here anymore.'

'You're running yourself into the ground right now.'

Conrad fingered the digestive, ready to go in for the last dunk when Edwina looked him in the eyes.

'I don't suppose you would... you know... maybe you and I...?'

If he'd had a mouthful of tea, it might have joined the wallpaper. 'What? Oh, Edwina, no, I'm sorry, that would be wholly inappropriate. Nothing personal, of course, but there's a line here that we can't cross. You have your mother's power of attorney, and I discuss her with you because you're her carer along with the hospice, but as for socialising... I'm sorry.'

Her cheeks went red. 'Yes, of course. I'm sorry. What was I thinking?' Tears again. He dunked the last bit of biscuit while she whipped out what used to be one of his hankies.

'It's fine. Honestly. I know emotions are running high just now, but somebody will come along and you'll be happy, I'm sure of it.'

He didn't want to mention that he was eight years her junior, and she was the last woman he'd want to spend a Friday night with.

'I just can't see the light at the end of the tunnel,' she said.

Conrad put the cup and saucer down on the side table and scooted forward. 'Are you online at all?' he asked her.

'What do you mean?'

'Do you go on the internet?' *Please tell me you've heard of the internet.*

'Of course I do. I use it to email.'

'Would you be interested in making new friends on there? Maybe in a support group. Meeting people who are in the same situation as you.'

Edwina took in a few deep breaths and waved a hand in front of her face. 'I don't know.'

'A lot of people do it nowadays.'

'There are a lot of killers on the internet. Psychos and stuff.'

'There are a lot of psychos in supermarkets too.'

'I wouldn't know, Kenneth. I don't talk to anybody in the supermarket.'

'I was just making a point. You could be standing next to one in the produce aisle. Or sitting next to one on the bus. Sometimes you just have to take a leap of faith.'

Edwina seemed to mull it over. 'Would Michael think it was a good idea?'

'I'm sure Doctor Salamin would think it an excellent idea.'

Edwina smiled. 'Right then. I'll do it. If you'll help me.'

'Tomorrow's Friday and I've nothing on. We'll get onto it after I check on your mother. How does that sound?'

'Sounds wonderful. I might even get some chocolate Hobnobs in.'

And that sealed the deal.

EIGHT

Jimmy Dunbar took a drink of water and sat back down. The room was silent, the faces looking at him.

'What next?' Jeni Bridge asked.

'By all accounts, Conrad told the investigators that he helped Edwina Adams contact a support group. She made friends with an older woman in the same position. They arranged to go out to lunch; as long as Conrad was there to stay with her mother, along with the hospice nurse. Which Conrad did, and we think that's when he took the opportunity to kill the old woman.'

Alex looked at him. 'Why would he kill her if she was already on her way out?'

Dunbar turned to look at her. 'He was finishing up as a doctor. He was only forty-five but felt he'd had enough, according to his colleagues who were interviewed. He wanted to buy a boat and sail round the world.'

'Boats are expensive,' Harry said, 'even on a GP's salary.'

Dunbar turned towards him. 'And that's why he needed money. And he knew how to get it. When we were talking to the partners in the surgery, they said that Conrad went above and beyond with Davina Adams. He insisted on going to see her every day, and we think the doctor was grooming the old woman.'

'Grooming her?' Jeni said, making a face.

'Oh, not like that, ma'am. Becoming her best friend. You see, Davina died a couple of days before Conrad retired. Nothing unusual, especially when a hospice nurse was also coming in. But a red flag was thrown up after the funeral had taken place and Edwina and her sister went to the solicitors to see about splitting up the house and their mother's estate. Turns out, the old woman had left everything to Conrad.'

'And that's what aroused suspicion,' Evans said.

'Exactly,' Dunbar said, carrying on. 'Edwina liked the good doctor a lot, and she knew her mother liked him too, but not enough to leave him her house and money. The old woman didn't have a lot of money in the bank, but the house itself was worth well over half a mil. As soon as the solicitor told them, they came to the police. A team from CID investigated. The old woman's body was exhumed and samples taken for toxicology and there were traces of fentanyl in her. Not unusual in a terminal situation like this one, but the old woman was already on morphine, and the nurse said she hadn't administered any fentanyl. The fact there was enough fentanyl in her system to kill an army was enough for the arrest warrant.'

'I had a quick skim through the report before we

came in here this afternoon, and saw that the doctor denied everything,' Jeni said.

'Correct. He was indignant, but when we searched his bag, there were traces of fentanyl inside, maybe a plastic bag had ripped and spilled some. It was enough to make the jury unanimous. That and hearing he was the one who had visited her the night she died.'

'Then CID went through all his patients. In his career, there were over a hundred old people who had died in his care,' Evans said. 'He denied any wrong doing, but they had three patients exhumed and all of them had traces of fentanyl in their system, enough to kill a bus load of them.'

Purcell looked at them. 'He was charged with the four deaths, because they was the only viable ones?'

'Yes, sir,' Dunbar said. 'That's why he was given a whole life sentence, because of the sheer number of suspected deaths.'

'And this afternoon, he escaped with Archie Higgins,' Jeni said. 'Are we working on the assumption that they concocted this together?'

'I wouldn't say so. There was no indication they ever hung out in Barlinnie. They were just being transported together for sentencing.'

'Conrad's escape might have just been opportunity,' Harry said.

Dunbar looked at him. 'I would say so. Where he would go, I have no idea. I have members of my team watching Higgins' house and family, and other places he might turn up, but time will tell. I personally don't think he'd be stupid enough to go back to Glasgow. If anything, he'll wait and have his wife meet him somewhere. Same with Conrad; I don't think he'll be going home any time soon.'

Jeni looked round the room. 'Right. I want the Edinburgh and Glasgow teams talking to each other. DCI Dunbar, make sure that happens. I don't want any mistakes made because nobody wanted to share. You will be based here with DCI McNeil since they escaped in our city. You have the authority to go wherever you need to, and with all resources at your disposal, including armed response. It would seem that both men are extremely dangerous, and we want them back in custody sooner rather than later.'

'Yes, ma'am.'

'You will use one of the incident rooms here. The other MITs are busy on other cases, but we'll have a task force put together, drafting in officers from CID and as many uniforms as you see fit. McNeil will be the lead on the investigation since this is his city, but rest assured, your input will be invaluable. Now, are there any other questions?'

There were none.

'Right. Read up on the reports. Each of you is representing one of our divisions so make sure all members of your area are briefed. Go get them.'

NINE

The temperature had dropped a little as they left the station and crossed the road. It was two minutes by foot to the courthouse.

'This Higgins is dangerous then, Jimmy?' Harry said.

'He is, but he's smart, like a sewer rat. I'd be more scared of coming up against Conrad in a dark alley. He's sneaky, somebody you think you can trust, then he's all over you.'

'You remember DS Eve Bell, Jimmy,' Harry said as they stood in the sunshine on The Mound. Dunbar nodded.

'This is DI Ronnie Vallance, the newest member.'

The two men nodded to each other like boxers waiting for the bell. Vallance was a big man; tall, not as tall as DC Simon Gregg, but well built. He had a bushy beard that was grey in parts, and hands like shovels.

'Good to meet you, Vallance.'

'Likewise, sir.'

They were looking at the detritus that had been left behind by the fire in the courthouse loading bay, including the burnt-out van sitting across St Giles Street. Fire engines were still present, their lights flashing and diesel engines grumbling. The fire commander came across to them when he spotted Harry.

'It's not as bad as it seems. Those vultures there,' he nodded to the press photographers who had stayed behind in a do-or-die mission, 'said that there was a lot of smoke, and I looked at some of the photographs. Some was from the fire, obviously, but we found a lot of used smoke grenades in there, which made it look ten times worse than it was.'

'And gave them plenty of cover as they made their escape,' Alex said.

'Indeed. They left by the other side and got away into the High Street because nobody came through the smoke. None of the photographers moved because not only was the van on fire, but two police cars were also torched. It was quite a show.'

'Anybody die inside there?' Robbie Evans asked, nodding to the blackened bay.

'No, thank God. They were knocked unconscious, but the main door was open so the smoke dissipated quickly. The door into the court itself was on fire but nothing that would have been life-threatening to the guards. Whoever set the fire didn't want to kill anybody and they obviously knew when the fire alarm was set off, there would be a fast response.'

'They did their homework,' Harry said.

'Oh yes. This was well planned.'

'Thanks,' Harry said. He looked at the burnt-out police vehicles. Uniforms were standing guard, keeping onlookers back, but The Mound had been closed to traffic.

'Now that your Mondeo is giving you trouble, you'd be better off with that thing,' Alex said to Harry, nodding at the burnt-out van.

'There's nothing wrong with my car.'

'Harry, darling, it's gone from, *We can bang that panel out a little bit, sir* to *Naw, pal, that's well fucked.*'

'Language, you wee besom. And it just needs a little bit of TLC.'

'It needs the last rites. You need a new car. That's all I'm saying.'

'We'll see.'

Harry stood looking into the dark void of what had been the prisoner receiving area and walked in out of the sunshine, his eyes adjusting to the gloom. Alex was by his side. Forensics teams were inside with firefighters, the whole place a charred ruin.

'Lucky nobody was killed in this,' she said.

'Luck had nothing to do with it,' Harry said. 'If Higgins had wanted them dead, I'm sure they would be dead.'

DI Maggie Parks, head of the unit, was there.

'The men were brought out and taken to the hospital. No serious injuries but they'll all have a headache,' she said.

'It wasn't his intent to kill them, just to escape, looks

44

like,' Harry said, glancing over at the charred office on the left.

'There are empty smoke grenades all over the place. They give off a hell of lot of smoke, making it look like the place was well alight.'

'It was less risky for them, making it look like it was engulfed. It was quite clever when you think about it.'

'You say that like you admire them, sir,' Maggie said.

'I admire their ingenuity. But they'll slip up. Then we'll get them. It seems that the security guards who were transporting them were in on it, so we have to trace them.'

'It was very well organised. I read about Archie Higgins. Quite the big shot through in Glasgow, isn't he?' Maggie said.

'He is. We have a team through from Glasgow to advise us on him and the doctor.'

'I think he's the one I'd be more scared of,' Maggie said, turning back to her crew.

Dunbar and Evans strolled over from outside. 'We've been talking to some of the photographers who took photos. The smoke was belching out and it provided a smokescreen, but they heard the sound of motorbikes taking off. Away from them. I know the team are checking CCTV so I'm sure we'll see some bikers waiting for the others to come out.'

'I wonder if Conrad got on one?' Alex said.

'I doubt it,' Dunbar said. 'I might be wrong, but I can't see Higgins getting Conrad involved. I think Conrad escaping was him seeing the opportunity and seizing it.'

'Agreed,' Harry said, 'but hopefully we'll have spotted him making off. See where he went. But let's go and talk to that security company. I want to give somebody a roasting.'

'We'll go back to the station, Harry,' Dunbar said. 'I want to contact my crew back home.'

'We'll go with you before heading out to the Gyle. My car's in the garage right now.'

'On its way to the scrapyard in the sky,' Alex added.

TEN

Kenneth Conrad didn't normally wear hats but he had swiped some old codger's hat off the overhead rack as the Glasgow train pulled into Edinburgh Park. He'd also grabbed a lightweight jacket. Nobody batted an eye, thinking the jacket must have been his. It was busy with tourists so he didn't stick out.

He'd been through here before, years back, and knew the train stopped here, opposite Hermiston Gait retail park. He knew there was a Tesco there too, one of the big ones that sold everything.

He made his way over to jackets and bought a rain-coat in navy blue. Something with a hood. And a cheap watch.

He wandered through the food aisles with his basket, grabbing some snacks for the time being, and then headed over to the electronics aisle where he picked up a dispos-able phone.

He paid in cash, not wanting to say much to the girl

at the till who obviously wasn't in the mood for conversation anyway. She was clearly working on her jaw exercises with the help of some gum.

After checking out, he unwrapped a pasty and ate it as he strolled back down to the road. He ditched the stolen hat, took his new one out of the bag, and put it on, then crossed over the road and waited for the tram to take him into the city centre. He paid the conductor for his ticket, harking back to the days when he was a small boy in Glasgow and his mother would tell him all about the clippies they had on the buses. He felt like he had gone back in time, with a clippie issuing him with a ticket now.

He sat back, not noticing the man who had been following him since leaving Waverley. That man too had bought a hat, the exact same one as he had.

Conrad watched as Murrayfield rugby stadium went by on his left and half expected a horde of coppers to come running on at every stop, and smash him to the ground, but none came.

At Haymarket, he got off and went into the station and bought a ticket for the Fife line. He could have got the Glasgow train back from Edinburgh Park but chopping and changing would throw them off.

He stood on the platform with the rest of the travellers. Sirens cut through the air, and his heart beat a bit faster as he thought he might hear the screeching of tyres and the clunk of car doors being slammed.

Neither came. He didn't even hear any chatter about the escape from the people waiting on the platform. It was heaving now, commuters waiting to go home, knowing the train would already be half full as it left Waverley.

When it did come, he didn't push or shove but went with the flow, and stood near the doors as all the seats filled up. The next stop was South Gyle where *all the fucking Gylies get off* as one woman put it.

The small crowd that got off didn't leave a dent in the seating availability but Conrad didn't mind standing. He'd been sitting for a long time today anyway.

As the train pulled away from South Gyle station, he squeezed by some people and went into the toilet. He took the throwaway phone out of the carrier bag and got the box open. After setting it up, he took the card out of his pocket and looked at the number on the business card that was in amongst the money he had been given.

He put the card in his pocket. Instead of dialling the number written on it, he dialled another number, one he had committed to memory. He waited, thinking for a moment that it wasn't going to be answered at the other end. Until it was.

'Yeah?'

'It's me,' he said. 'I need your help.' Then the voice told him what to do next.

ELEVEN

The incident room was full of bodies buzzing about, men and women on telephones, sitting at computers and, pinning things on a board.

'We've had sightings everywhere from John O'Groats to a local playground,' DI Ronnie Vallance said, coming across to Harry.

'Narrow it down to the semi-feasible ones for now, Ronnie,' Harry replied. 'Any results from CCTV on the motorbikes?'

'We got them on camera in the High Street. DI Shiels is heading a small team to try and track them.'

They walked over to Karen Shiels. 'What's the latest, Karen?'

'There were six bikes heading out of St Giles Street and into the High Street. We tapped into the council cameras. We're not a hundred per cent sure it's them as they all had leather jackets and helmets on, but we're working on that theory. There are sightings of them on surrounding cameras.'

'Number plates, ma'am?' Robbie Evans asked.

'Believe it or not, we did get clear shots of them all. They're fake. They look like they're magnetic fakes slapped on, which means they could have been taken off around the corner.'

'What's the assumption?' Alex asked. 'That the keys were left in the bikes for them?'

'Yes. With somebody guarding them of course.'

'Keep on checking the CCTV,' Harry said. 'I'm going out to the Edinburgh depot of Armour Security, while DCI Dunbar talks with his DI through in the west; he's been talking to the Glasgow depot where the guards were stationed. They're all gone so we're working on the theory that they were working for Higgins.' He turned to Vallance.

'Ronnie, make sure you follow up with any viable leads on sightings.'

'Will do, sir.'

'I'll get Robbie to Facetime with my DI now, Harry,' Dunbar said.

'See you downstairs in the car.'

Harry and Alex headed out to the car park where Alex's Audi was waiting.

'Now we own our own flat, things are heading in the right direction. Owning two cars isn't a problem for us. Everything will fall into place. You just need to start visiting car showrooms.'

'Now why would I want to go and spoil a nice

Saturday afternoon? Besides, I have you to drive me around.'

'You're not getting behind the wheel of this car, Harry McNeil. Your attempts at psychology are pathetic. *I have you to drive me around.* You want me to say, *I'm not driving you around anymore. Drive yourself.*'

'Can't fault a man for trying.'

He smiled at her. He'd met her a year earlier, and now they lived together and were heading for marriage further down the road. He couldn't have asked for a better wife.

Dunbar came down a few minutes later and got in the back. 'This is far better than Robbie's old clunker. I wish he'd spend his money on upgrading to something like this.'

'It's good to see you again, sir,' Alex said as they headed out to the west of the city. 'And young Robbie.'

'It's always good to get back through to Auld Reekie, Alex.'

'I suppose we'll be seeing you both in the bar later?'

'Only in the interests of comparing notes.'

'Comparing notes is what we do best,' Harry said.

South Gyle industrial estate was on the west side of the city. Easy escape for the hordes of Fifers who came through to the capital to work every day.

Alex turned left at the roundabout, where Ferranti the electronic manufacturer used to be. A Lightning Jet had sat on a pedestal in their grounds until the company left that location.

'Have you ever wondered what it would be like to

work nine-to-five in a place like this?' she asked as she followed the road round.

'It's alright for some, I suppose, but it's not for me.'

'I can't imagine spending the rest of my working life cooped up in a room, sitting in a little cubicle, answering phones and answering to some tyrant of a manager,' Dunbar said.

'Sounds like you just described working in our incident room.' She laughed.

'And who's the bloody tyrant boss?' Harry asked.

She slowed the car down as they approached the Armour Security depot. 'If the shoe fits...'

She turned left into a driveway that had a barrier across it. A man in uniform stepped out of the guard hut and approached. 'Help you?'

They held up their warrant cards.

'We need to speak to the manager of this place.'

'I wondered when you lot would turn up. But that van wasn't from our depot.'

'I never said it was,' Harry replied. 'Call ahead and tell somebody to meet us.'

The man walked away muttering under his breath, and went inside and pressed whatever button lifted the metal bar.

'You remember when this used to be Securicor Omega Express?' Harry said.

Alex looked puzzled. 'I was brought up in Fife, remember? I wouldn't know what was here.'

'I've never been to the moon, but I know where it is.'

'Nobody likes a smartarse, Harry,' Dunbar said. 'Especially when you're being one to your good lady.'

'Well, it was for your collection of useless trivia. They were a parcel delivery company, amongst other things. Other companies moved in after they left, but none of them survived. Then this crowd took over.'

'If I'm ever on *Who Wants to be a Millionaire*, you know you're not going to be my phone-a-friend.'

'Fine. Have Simon Gregg. Unless it's a football question, you'll be cuffed.'

'DCI Dunbar will gladly be my phone-a-friend.'

'Don't get me involved in all of this.'

She parked the car over on the right beside other cars and they got out.

The depot looked like a big warehouse, with roller doors all along the front, where the parcel trucks used to back in. This end, closest to the road, was the office block.

An intercom with video faced them at the entrance door. McNeil buzzed and they held up their warrant cards. The door was buzzed open and they walked in. A walled-off reception area greeted them, with a woman sitting behind a glass partition.

'DCI Harry McNeil, DCI Dunbar from Glasgow Division and DS Alex Maxwell. We'd like to speak to your manager, or whoever is in charge of this facility.'

'That'll be Mr Wiley. I'll tell him you're here if you'd like to take a seat.'

They looked at the uncomfortable hard plastic chairs and elected to stand.

The woman got on the phone and a few minutes

later, a balding man with a sweaty forehead opened the door and poked his head round.

'Come this way,' he said.

'Mr Wiley?' Harry asked.

'Aye, that's me. But I'll no' be the manager for too much longer. This was an almighty cock-up today.'

'Isn't this a new company?' Alex asked.

'Aye. Been on the go for a couple of months now, but you know what it's like with some places; they promise you the earth, and as soon as you become staff, you realise they were talking out their arse.'

'Was this place started from scratch, the prison gig, I mean? Or was it an offshoot of a larger company?'

'Larger company. Armour Holdings. They have Armour this and Armour that. They supply those old guys who sit at the front desk of office buildings, that sort of thing. Loads of other security stuff, of course. In here.'

He led them into an office that had a view of the car park.

'Grab a pew. Let's talk while we can. The divisional manager is on his way over, probably to give me my jotters, but to hell with them.' He watched as Harry and Alex took a seat before sitting down at his desk. Dunbar stood by the door, as if he didn't trust the man not to do a runner.

'You know, I worked my way up in this company. I started off as a doorman, sitting in reception after reception, before moving into the armoured truck division. Then I became a manager, and then some bright spark upstairs decided to put a bid in for the prison transport tender, and we won it. That was months ago. That gave us time to get all the necessary vehicles. The company invested a lot of money.'

'Invested a lot of money in personnel too, I'll bet,' Alex said.

Wiley shook his head and put a hand over his eyes for a second. 'Bastards.' Then he took his hand away and looked at them. 'Oh, not you. Those bastards that worked in the Glasgow depot. They were interviewed here, this being the Scottish HQ. I have their names on file, ready to give you any help you need.'

Wiley took some papers from a letter tray and passed them over to Harry.

'Six of them. All from Glasgow, but they interviewed here, as I said. Me and the HR manager gave the go ahead.'

Harry looked at each page before handing the paper over to Dunbar. 'Nothing seemed out of the ordinary when they interviewed?'

Wiley shook his head. 'The opposite; they were exemplary. A whole bunch came through on a bus for interviewing. We had to weed out the no-hopers and time was of the essence. Those six were ex-army. They had all the paper, by God. They held up very well. This was for the second, serious round of interviews. They had the numpties weeded out locally, but this was a case of the ones who could genuinely do the job. Most of the bus load got through. But those six, well, the depot manager through in Glasgow put in a word for them. He told me they were excellent candidates and to pay special attention to them. They came recommended by the west regional manager.'

'Do you know this regional manager who recommended them?' Dunbar asked.

Wiley looked pained. 'No. I never heard of him before this prison malarkey started. Crow's his name. Sounds like a bloody crow too if you ask me.'

'Have you had any contact with him today since the escape?' Alex asked.

They could almost see the little lightbulb go off in his head. 'No. I was in touch with the Glasgow depot, talking to my counterpart there, but I never deal with the west regional manager, only my own, here in the east. There's three of them, the other one being in the north.'

Harry looked at the last sheet and passed it over to Dunbar, who in turn was passing them to Alex.

'Tell me how all this prisoner transport stuff works, Mr Wiley. I don't know the ins and outs, other than they turn up at court in one of your vans,' Dunbar said.

'Okay. There would be six of them in the van, leaving the Glasgow depot. They would drive to Barlinnie, pick up the prisoners for transport and take them to the court here in Edinburgh. Two guards in the front, four in the back, two to each man. Because they were high profile. If it was just some wee jakie, there would be one to each man.'

'Right. The van gets to court and drops them off, but where would it wait? The loading bay is only big enough for one van,' Harry said.

'Normally, outside. But if it's going to be an all-day

affair, then it would come here and bide its time. Then when the prisoners were done with, they would be in the holding cells until their assigned van got back.'

'Is that what happened today?' Alex asked.

'Yes. The van came back here, but the driver reported some fault with it, so it was swapped out. They took a spare for the pickup. We had it waiting for them when they got here.'

'Was it a van designated a spare, or do you just pull one from the fleet?' Harry asked.

'It's a spare. All the others are out on regular runs, but we keep two spare. If three broke down, we'd get one from another depot. But this was one of our spares, prepared for going out in the afternoon on the Higgins' pickup.'

'Obviously, you know who you're picking up and transporting at all times,' Alex said. 'I mean, the guards know who they're transporting. They drop off the prisoners and take the same ones back.'

'Oh yes. Whoever picks them up, takes them back.'

'Do you know what the problem was with the van that was swapped?'

'I can look it up.' Wiley worked his keyboard at the computer. 'Transmission not shifting right. The driver was worried about it breaking down since they were travelling through to Glasgow and they didn't want it breaking down on the motorway.'

'I'd like to keep those sheets with the guards' information on them,' Harry said.

'They're yours.'

'I'd also like to speak with the mechanic who worked on the van that came in.'

'I'll take you along to the end where the mechanics are located. While I still have a job.'

'I wouldn't worry, Mr Wiley,' Harry said as they all stood up. 'This wasn't your fault.'

'I know that, but the buck has to stop somewhere.'

They left the office and took a different corridor from the one they'd come in along, and they went through a door into the warehouse.

'This used to be the sorting facility for Securicor,' Wiley said. 'Many years ago before they were bought out by a German company and integrated into DHL.'

'I was telling DS Maxwell that. I remember it being here.'

They walked through the cavernous area where some vans were parked, until they reached the far end, then went through a door that led into a spacious area where the vehicles were worked on.

'Bobby!' Mr Wiley shouted.

A burly man wearing a uniform with oil stains on it, came across, wiping his hands on a rag.

'A'right, boss?'

Wiley introduced the three detectives. 'Who worked on that van that reported a fault? The Glasgow one?'

'That was wee Benny.'

'Has he worked on it yet?' Wiley asked.

'Not yet. It's sitting over there.' The man had finished wiping his hands and nodded towards the open door where the vehicles backed in.

'Did he prepare the one that went out?'

'Aye, he did. And I chewed him a new one for it.'

'Why was that?' Dunbar asked.

The man looked at him. 'Benny hasn't worked with us that long. He's a good worker, don't get me wrong, but he's a bit of a slow worker. Like this morning; prepping one of the spare vans should take half an hour. Making sure all the fluids are level, then take it for a drive, make sure it's okay. But that wee sod spent a couple of hours on it. I hadn't realised until I needed him for something else.'

'Did you make sure the van was okay before it left for the pickup?' Alex asked.

Bobby shook his head. 'Too busy. Besides, it's a basic job. Nobody could mess that up.'

Harry nodded. 'Okay. Thanks for that. But I'd like that Glasgow van left alone. I'm having it impounded. Make sure nobody touches it.'

'Nae bother.'

They walked through the large roller door into the sunshine.

'You think Benny tampered with the van?' Wiley asked.

'I'm saying we need to rule it out,' Harry said. 'I'm going to need his details.'

'Sure. I'll get them for you.'

Ten minutes later, they were back in the car. Harry got on the radio while Alex drove.

'Ronnie? It's Harry. Get over to Clovenstone with uniforms and an armed team. We're going to an address and we don't want to be caught short. I'll wait near there and text you my position. Then we go in heavy-handed.'

'Okay, boss.'

Dunbar got on his own phone and spoke to one of his DIs. Told him what they'd just discovered.

Alex drove through South Gyle up to Clovenstone. 'You think this Benny bloke might be hiding Archie Higgins?'

'He might very well be. At the very least, I think he did something to that van to make it go up like that. Rigged something up in it to set it on fire.'

'This was very well planned. But I can't see them being this stupid, hanging about in Benny's place.'

'Me neither. But it's a lead.'

TWELVE

'It didn't take you lot long to come round here,' Candy Higgins said, stepping back and letting the police team in.

'This is a search warrant, Mrs Higgins,' DI Tom Barclay said, holding out the piece of paper. DS Adrian Wells was with him.

The house was large, far removed from the ordinary family homes in Govan, where he was stationed.

'You don't need a warrant, he isn't here. Look at anything you want.'

'Let's just make it official, Mrs Higgins.'

'We wouldn't want to upset DCI Dunbar now, would we?'

'No, you wouldn't.'

The swarm of uniforms made their way through the house, bagging up computers and iPads and papers. Anything that might tell them where her husband could be.

Two hours later, Barclay stood outside on the phone to his boss. 'We took the computers, boss. And other stuff. But he's not hiding up in the attic or in the garden hut. They have two cars registered in their names and they're both here.'

'Keep on it, son. And get those computers through to the labs right away. Make sure they know the urgency of the matter.'

'Will do.' He hung up and the crowd of uniforms dispersed to their vehicles. Barclay walked over to Candy Higgins, who was standing at the door watching them.

'We'll have a car sitting outside, twenty-four seven,' he said to her.

'I have no doubt.' She stepped away from him and closed the door.

Barclay got in the car with Wells. 'Back to the station so we can interview the manager of the Armour transport depot. Let's see what fairy stories he has for us.'

'I have a bad feeling about this,' Alex said, adjusting her stab-proof vest. She was standing behind her car with Harry who was similarly attired.

'You and me both. I asked Ronnie to double-check and he just got back to me; Benny doesn't exist. His paper trail was false.'

'It's no coincidence that this manager called Crow in Glasgow recommended Benny and the guards who were escorting Higgins,' Dunbar said.

'I know.'

The uniforms were in position with the ram. Nobody who had ever been on a raid like this was taking a chance. Harry looked over at the entry team and held up a fist. Then brought it down sharply and immediately Benny's door was off its hinges and the armed team were in.

Shouts. Screams. Promises of bodily harm should the occupant decide to come out fighting. Moments later, the armed team came back out informing Harry the house was clear.

They went in, with uniforms following close behind.

'It's empty, sir,' one of the uniformed sergeants said. The door had pushed a pile of mail back and Harry pulled on a pair of nitrile gloves and picked some of it up. He rifled through it; the pile consisted of mostly junk mail but there were a few letters, addressed to a woman.

'She's listed as the previous tenant, DI Vallance told me,' he said.

'There's nothing to indicate anybody lived here after that woman,' Alex said.

Harry turned to the sergeant. 'Get bodies knocking on doors. I want to know who neighbours saw coming and going. I'll have the Armour company send over a photo of this Benny guy from his file so you can start showing them.'

'Yes, sir.' The uniform walked out of the house while Harry got on the phone to Mr Wiley to ask for the photo.

'Pound to a penny this Benny bloke doesn't exist. And he was working for Higgins,' Dunbar said.

'That would make sense; the driver reports a fake

fault with the van, and then Benny rigs up one of the spares.'

'Jeni Bridge is not going to be a happy camper,' Alex said.

'I'm glad you'll be the one telling her.'

'Yeah, watch me. That job is for you and DCI Dunbar.'

'The shit always runs downhill, just remember that, sergeant,' Dunbar said with a grin.

THIRTEEN

'We weren't expecting you until tomorrow,' the man said, opening the door wider.

'It's all part of the service,' the doctor said. 'We don't want your mother to be in pain now, do we?'

'No, of course not.'

'I'm Doctor Conrad.' The doctor was wearing a hat, and a scarf that came up onto his face, covering his mouth and nose.

The man nodded. If his eyes had widened on recognition of the name, his life would have ended at that moment, but if he did recognise it, he hid it very well.

'I'm going to need you to run to the chemist to get some stuff. Like a tub of chest rub. That will help her breathe a bit better,' the doctor said.

The man, who was the old woman's son, looked confused for a moment, and the doctor thought he was going to argue. But then he nodded.

'I'll just get my coat, doctor.'

'Sure, no hurry.' *Any fucking time today.*

The man went into the living room where the woman was. 'I'm going out, Ma. The doctor is here. He's just checking up on you.'

'Okay, son.' The woman's voice was old and feeble.

The man grabbed his jacket. The doctor looked at him in disgust. He had looked at the file; he was in his forties, never been married, lived with his mother. Obviously attracting a member of the opposite sex was the last thing on his mind, considering the pullover he was wearing. One of those sleeveless things. And a shirt and tie! What the fuck was all that about?

'I won't be long.' He stood looking at the doctor for a second. Wondering why he hadn't taken his hat or scarf off but not wanting to ask. Well, he did, but not really.

'Okay, that's good. I don't have that much time, so if you can be there and back again as soon as, that would be super.'

'Right then, I'll be off.'

Right then, fuck off. The doctor stared at him until he moved. That always seemed to do the trick; stare at them, make them move.

The son left and the doctor waited until he heard the door close.

'Where's my son?' she asked.

'He's away to the chemist.'

'Is he coming back?'

'He'll be coming back shortly.'

'He hasn't left me here all alone, has he?'

And then the doctor knew how the son's life had

been fucked. The overpowering mother, the guilt that had probably been piled on him. Stay home, look after Mother.

'I don't want you getting excited. Just you sit back. I heard you've been in a bit of pain.'

'I fell.'

'Do you have any other children, Mrs Mackay?'

'Yes. I have a daughter. She's married with kids. Very busy but she said she'll try and get up next week to see me. Bring the kids with her.'

'How long has it been since you saw your grandchildren?'

'Oh, just last week, son. Or last month. Oh, I don't really know.'

'Well, I'm going to give you something that will take the pain away.'

'I'm afraid of needles, doctor.'

'This won't hurt much at all. Just a little prick.' *Like your son.*

He brought the needle out, holding it a gloved hand, and rolled the woman's sleeve up. He injected her. He watched her eyes glaze over for a second then he put his gloved hand on her neck and squeezed hard. She wouldn't be able to fight back and scratch him, but he had to leave his mark, so the death would be suspicious. She slumped over. Death wouldn't be long.

He closed his doctor's bag, holding the syringe in one hand after he'd wiped it and put gloves on. He sat and waited for the son to come back.

Fifteen minutes later, he heard the front door being

opened. He stood up, making sure the scarf was still covering his face then handed the syringe to the son.

'You can dispose of that in your rubbish bin.'

'Is that right, for people to throw away the syringe in the rubbish?'

'Oh, yes. It's the new rule. I can't put a syringe back in my bag after administering a drug to a patient. Cross contamination, you see. And this isn't medical waste, just a syringe.'

'Oh, okay.' He took it and walked into the kitchen and threw it in the rubbish bin.

The doctor walked out of the house, closing the door quietly behind him. They would find the syringe in the rubbish with some morphine still in it, so there would be no doubt.

He went to a phone box, one of the few still around these days, and dialled 999.

He put on a gruff voice, talking through his scarf. 'I think my neighbour killed his mother. I saw him injecting her with something. I'm scared. I think he's going to kill me next.' He gave the address and hung up.

Walked away along the road to where the car was waiting.

FOURTEEN

'Remember the night you were in here with Frank Miller and you were trying to avoid me?' Alex said with a grin before she sipped her Diet Coke.

'Vaguely.'

'I saw you and was going to crash your wee party with Frank until he called me over. Now you don't have to hide.'

'I wasn't hiding. I was avoiding you. There's a difference.'

'Now I'm your live-in lover so there's no hiding.'

'God, you make it sound like something from a Victorian novel.'

She grinned as the door to the St Bernard's pub opened and Jimmy Dunbar walked in with Robbie Evans.

'I actually missed this wee boozer,' Evans said as they approached Harry's table.

'Well, how's about recalling what it's like to buy a round?' Dunbar said.

Harry laughed. 'Sit down both of you, this is on me.' He stepped up to the bar and got the drinks in before sitting back down.

'Right, Harry,' Dunbar said after taking a drink from his pint glass. 'I had a wee conference call with my team back in Govan. We're sending uniforms round to all known locations where Higgins has family and known associates. Hopefully, at the same time, so we're carpet bombing them. So far, there's nothing. My DI, a bloke you would like, Tom Barclay, told me that he went to speak with this joker called Crow at the Glasgow depot of Armour Security, and guess what?'

'He doesn't exist.'

'Correct. Oh, he had been there alright. Strutted about the place like he owned it, according to the other workers, but every credential he had was fake. He was long gone by the time Barclay got there.'

'Brilliant though,' Evans added. 'Whoever is responsible for all the fake IDs knows his stuff.'

'Higgins had this well planned,' Alex added.

'How about your team, Harry?' Dunbar asked.

'While you were having your teleconference call, one of my team captured Conrad on CCTV going into Waverley Station. They tracked him onto the Glasgow train.'

'How did he pay for his ticket?'

'Cash. He must have got it from one of Higgins' men.

But we checked the CCTV from Glasgow Queen Street, and he didn't get off. So we checked the stations from Waverley, starting at Haymarket, and we got him at Hermiston Gait, a small shopping place on the west side of Edinburgh. They checked feed from around there and he went into Tesco and caught the tram back to Haymarket, then went into the station and hopped on the Fife train. He got off at Lochgelly and that was the last we've seen of him. We got Fife to swarm the place and we've put out a notice, but he could have gone anywhere. We checked the information we have, and he has no connection to the village.'

'We'll keep looking. Somebody must have seen something,' Dunbar said.

'We know what clothes he bought, but that doesn't mean anything. He could hit a charity shop and buy some stuff. He could have changed several times by now and we wouldn't know what he was wearing,' Alex said.

'I'll get my team to check and see if Higgins has any connection to Fife, but I don't think he has.' Dunbar drank some of his pint. 'I wonder why he would give Conrad money?'

'Maybe Higgins just felt sorry for him and wanted to help,' Evans said.

Harry thought for a moment. 'I think it's more than that; it must have been intense in there, with the van on fire and smoke belching everywhere. Higgins wouldn't have wanted to hang around. But he stopped one of his men to give Conrad money. No, I think there's something more going on, something we don't know about yet.'

'They'll slip up sooner or later and then we'll get

them,' Dunbar said. 'But did you know, young Robbie here is wenching?'

'Oh, Jesus, here we go,' Evans said.

'And, believe it or not, it's not my sister-in-law.'

'I told you in confidence.' Evans hid his reddening face behind his pint glass.

'What are you worried about, son? These are our Edinburgh friends. They won't knock the piss out of you.'

'There's nothing to knock.'

'She's better than the last one he had. She came in a box and he was out of breath by the time he'd fully inflated her.'

'Give it a rest.'

Harry laughed.

'Tell us more, Robbie,' Alex said.

'We met online. She's American. Nothing serious.'

'Does that mean your days of nightclubs are over?' Harry asked.

'For the time being. She's nice.'

'I never thought I'd hear the day,' Dunbar said. 'Always out on the randan, and now he's found a lassie who's tying a ball and chain round his ankle. Is this the real Evans we're talking to?'

'It was bound to happen one day,' Harry said.

'You should see him; they're always doing that snap talking or something.'

'Snapchat, grandad.'

Dunbar laughed. 'Bloody putting comic faces on their photos. Mind you, I can see Robbie wanting to hide his ugly mug behind a spaniel's ears. But that lassie's a looker, she doesn't need to hide her face.'

'That's not the point of it. Alex knows what I'm talking about. Why don't you explain it to Uncle Jimmy there, who was brought up sitting round the tranny as somebody tried to tune in to Glen Miller.'

'Who's Glen Miller?' Dunbar asked.

'Yeah, right. You fine well know who he is.'

'Let's not forget all the texting he does as well. I'm lucky if I can get him to write a report these days. I should get him to text his reports, then they'd soon get done.'

'I can see it's slag-off Robbie Evans day. Anybody else ready for a top-up?'

They all agreed they were.

'I'll help you,' Alex said.

Up at the bar, they waited to get hold of the barman.

'What about you, Alex? Have you and Harry decided on a date yet?'

'We're not engaged yet. We only just bought the flat.'

'I don't know what he's waiting for. If I was him, I wouldn't want anybody to swoop in and steal my girl-friend. I'd be putting a ring on your finger sharpish.'

Alex laughed. 'Harry doesn't have to worry about me going anywhere.'

'I know. Just keep him on his toes.'

They collected the drinks and returned to the table.

'What about you, sir?' Evans said. 'Have you and Alex set a date for getting married?' He looked inno-cently at Harry and gave Alex a sly wink.

'Er, well, no, not yet, although...' He didn't finish his sentence. 'Soon.'

'He just wants to show off his new girlfriend at your wedding, if she can hop on a plane from Boston,' Dunbar said. 'Some people will do anything for a free meal.'

FIFTEEN

Candy Higgins sat in the dark, feeling exhausted. Those police were such bastards. She didn't really blame DI Barclay, or Jimmy Dunbar come to that, but why did they always assume the worst?

Because they know he'll come back here.

She had to admit that she thought they were right. As soon as he could, Archie would make his way back home, but were the police that stupid to think he would come here right away? Clearly.

He would make contact with her. Somehow. The phones would be tapped, but they would get round that by getting burner phones.

She knocked back some of the wine, the expensive red stuff that Archie liked. She had gone and bought some when Eddie had come round to tell her Archie had escaped.

She put the glass down on the table in front of her and picked up the remote for the TV. A million emotions were running through her just now: anger, fear, excitement, jealousy. She was angry that the police had been to her door again, scared that Archie would get caught before she could see him again, excited at the prospect of holding him, and jealous of the fact that Eddie knew what was happening and her husband had kept her out of the loop.

She flipped stations, not really paying attention to anything in particular. She'd muted it earlier and kept the sound off.

Rebecca would be so proud of her dad for sticking it up the authorities. She smiled, then the wave of sadness hit her. Her daughters were her whole life and now one of them was gone. The things she had planned to do with Becca. Turning sixteen had meant she was a young lady, on the cusp of womanhood. They would be friends as well as mother and daughter.

Now it was all gone. And Archie was gone because he'd been stupid enough to murder Becca's killer. And got caught. Now she didn't have her daughter or her—

The sound was small but distinct.

The back door had opened.

The living room was large, and French doors led through to their huge kitchen where a picture window looked out onto the back garden. Normally, she would have been alerted by the security floodlights coming on, but she had switched them off earlier, just in case Archie had been stupid enough to try and come home tonight.

Maybe she had been wrong about him. Maybe he

was missing her so much, he would risk everything to be with her.

The TV was still on mute and she listened intently. The door didn't squeak, but she heard a little click as it was closed. The living room was in darkness, only illuminated by the TV.

She sat stock still, her back against the settee. What if the police were watching, or had bugged the house as well as the phone? If she kept the lights off, then they wouldn't notice any change, and Archie could come in and they wouldn't be any the wiser.

She saw a shadow moving in the kitchen. Oh God, this was it.

The handle on the living room door clicked as it turned.

The door opened almost silently.

The soft rustle of feet on the thick carpet.

She sensed him right behind her now.

'Hello, Candy.'

Before she had a chance to scream, he swung his fist into her face.

SIXTEEN

Outside the St Bernard's, they started strolling towards the hotel further along, the same one where Dunbar and Evans had stayed a few months earlier when they had been working on a case together.

The two DCIs walked behind the sergeants.

'How you been holding up since your mother passed?' Dunbar asked.

'It's been a couple of months, and still I sometimes go to call her and then I remember she's gone.'

'My old dear's been gone for ten years and I miss her every fucking day. Bastard cancer took her. My old man was devastated and kept talking about wanting God to take him. He lasted three years before he had a heart attack. It's a bitch, Harry.'

'It feels... I dunno... weird.'

'Like you're an orphan now, even although you're a grown man.'

'Exactly. I know it's going to take time but...'

'Time doesn't heal, pal, it just eases the pain a wee bit.'

'My son, Chance, is taking it hard. He just turned seventeen, and he's had it rough this past few years since me and his mother split up. He sometimes went to stay with my mum. Just to get away from his mother.'

'Does he come and stay with you?'

'He hasn't so far, but he loves Alex and he said he'll come and spend a weekend soon.'

They were getting nearer the hotel. 'You're a lucky man, Harry. That lassie is not only a great woman to have in your life, but she's a spot-on detective. No' like heid the baw there.'

Harry laughed. 'Robbie's fine. He'll make a good inspector one day.'

'No doubt, but I can see Alex going to the top.'

'Me too.'

'Any problems from her ex?'

'None at all. I'm surprised, but I think coming face to face with you two put the wind up him.'

'Any hassle from him, give me a call, mind. You get an alibi and me and the lad will talk to the bastard.'

'Let's hope it doesn't come to that.'

They reached the hotel.

'He's probably going to go up and show his girlfriend photos of himself,' Dunbar said, his voice getting louder. 'What do you call them again?'

'I'm not even listening to you,' Evans said. 'I'm going to raid the minibar since it's on Glasgow Division.'

'Don't you be getting tanked up, ya wee sod. Get to your scratcher and whatever it is you're going to send photos of, keep it clean. I don't want any reports from vice.'

'Good God. We're not teenagers.'

'Alex, I hope that laddie hasn't corrupted you.'

'I'm fine, sir. I kept him in check.'

Evans shook his head. 'Sir, I think Scooby's waiting for his nightly chit-chat with you on Facetime.'

'I'm that dug's whole world. He's going to miss his dad.' Dunbar turned to Harry. 'You should get a dog, Harry. A big Rottweiler and set it about Evans when he comes here and gives you lip.'

'I don't need a Rottweiler when I've got...' he looked at Alex, who was standing with her eyebrows raised. 'This is going to go downhill fast, so I'll bid you both goodnight. See you in the morning.'

'Night, Harry. Alex.' Dunbar turned to Evans. 'Get right up to bed. I don't want to be waking you in the morning.'

'Make it sound like we're sharing a room, why don't you?'

'You should be so lucky.'

Harry and Alex crossed the road as the other two detectives went into the hotel.

'We are going to invite them to our wedding, if you ever get round to proposing, aren't we?'

Harry stopped on one of the landings. '*When* we get round to it. We should talk about that when we get in.'

Mia, their next-door neighbour across the landing, opened her door when they arrived.

'Oh, I'm sorry. I'm expecting somebody. I thought that was him now.'

'Hi, Mia,' Alex said, crouching to pet the cat as he came running out. 'Hey, Sylvester.'

'And here's me thinking you were just being nosy,' Harry said.

'Cheeky. But I think he knows me too well, by now, eh, Alex?'

'I would say so.' They both laughed and the cat went scurrying into the flat.

'See you around,' she said, closing the door behind her.

Inside the flat, as Harry put the kettle on for their nightly cup of green tea the phone rang.

'Hello?'

'*It's me, Dad,*' Chance McNeil said.

'Hello, son.'

'*Can we Facetime?*'

'Sure. Everything okay?'

'*Yeah.*'

'Okay, let me go to the bedroom. I'll just be a minute.' He winked at Alex and she gave him the thumbs-up. He took the phone into the room and the Facetime rang.

'Hi, pal, what's up?' He sat on the bed holding his phone so his own face appeared in the right-hand corner.

'I just had another fight with Mum. God Almighty, Dad, she's getting on my case now. She never lets up.'

'What have you been up to?' There was never any smoke without fire.

'Nothing. Honest.'

'Come on, Chance. It's me you're talking to. I might be an old fart, but I was young once.'

'You're hardly old at forty, Dad. Oldish.'

'So why is the dragon getting on your case?'

'Coming in late,' Chance said, sneaking a look over his shoulder to check that nobody was listening. 'It's not so much her as that arsehole she's going out with. He chips in with his opinion. I hate it here.'

'Why don't you come and spend some time here? You're on holiday from school.'

'Tam said I couldn't.'

'He's nothing to do with your life. If I say it's okay, then it's okay.'

'He gets blootered all the time, then he starts getting aggressive.'

'Has he ever laid his hand on you?'

The hesitation was the only answer Harry needed.

'When?' was all he said.

'Look, I didn't tell you this to cause a scene, but he grabbed a hold of me one night and slammed me up against the wall. He was going to punch me but Mum interrupted him. They had a row about it.'

'Has he done it since?'

Chance couldn't look at his father. 'Twice. You know, Dad, I don't want to bother you, but when Tam started his nonsense, I would usually have just driven down to Grandma's house. I really miss doing that.'

'I know, son. I miss her too. But if you don't want to come here, you could always drive down to see Uncle Derek. He and Briony are there. It's the same house and they would welcome you.'

'You don't think they would see me as a pest?'

'Of course not, son. I'll call Derek and make sure he knows you're coming.'

'Thanks, Dad. I just want to get out of the house for a little while.'

'I can also call Tam and let him know he's on borrowed time.'

'No, Dad, I don't want any trouble. I have to live here.'

Harry looked at his son and felt a wave of guilt wash over him. What if he'd made a better go of his marriage? What if they hadn't got divorced? But then a little voice in his head reminded him the divorce wasn't his idea in the first place.

'Let me call him. Just you get in that little boneshaker of yours and get down to Dalgety Bay.'

'Okay, I will. Thanks, Dad.'

Chance cut the Facetime call and Harry called his brother. 'Derek? It's me, your older and wiser brother, not to mention better looking.'

'What? Delusional, maybe.'

They both laughed. Harry was amazed at what a couple of months and losing their mother could do for their relationship. He hadn't spoken to his brother for years, up until a few months ago.

'Listen, Derek, Chance called me asking if it would be okay for him to come down and see you. Spend some time with you. Tam's been giving him a hard time. Physically hurting him as well.'

'What? That fat bastard. He thinks he's hard because his family are a shower of scum buckets. Of course tell the laddie he can come here. He can stay as long as he wants, Harry. He's flesh and blood and Briony won't mind.'

'Just keep an eye on him for me, Derek. And if Tam gives you any nonsense, call me.'

'Will do, bro.'

Harry hated it when his brother called him *bro* but let it slide. They said their goodbyes and Harry went back to the living room.

'Everything okay?' Alex asked.

Harry explained what was going on.

'That Tam sounds like a real charmer,' she said.

'His whole family are scum. I need to have a talk with him about putting his hands on my laddie.'

'I wonder if Morag knows?'

'It wouldn't surprise me. I'll need to ask her.'

'Don't, Harry,' she replied, putting her tea down on the coffee table. 'You might make it worse for Chance.'

'Aye, maybe you're right. I said he could come and stay here any time he wants. Just for a wee break.'

'Fine by me. I think the world of him. He can stay with us anytime.'

'Thanks, love.' He sat down and kissed her.

They watched a bit of TV before heading to bed. Harry's thoughts were on two murderers running loose and one lowlife who had dared to touch his little boy. He wasn't sure what made him more angry.

SEVENTEEN

Thunder cracked overhead and the sky unleashed its fury on the city. The rain battered off Jessfield House care home, lashing off the windows.

'Jesus, listen to that buckin weather outside,' Mary, one of the nursing assistants said.

'I'm glad we're on night shift,' Ruby said. She was happy to be at work so she wouldn't have to listen to her husband coming in drunk again, staggering about the house as he tried to get undressed for bed, thinking he was in any fit state to have his way with her.

'Me too. It's much quieter when they're sleeping.'

They were in the front office having a cup of tea and didn't notice the man standing in the open doorway at first.

'Oh Christ,' Ruby said as a flash of lightning lit up the black sky. 'You gave us a fright standing there,' she said. 'Visiting hours are over, pal. Come back tomorrow.'

He was wearing an old-fashioned hat, which was soaked. Water ran off onto his long raincoat.

'I'm not here visiting,' he said, his eyes boring into them.

'Then what *are* you here for?' Ruby said, barely disguising the contempt in her voice. This was their cuppa time and who was he to interrupt it?

'My name is DI Tom Barclay from Police Scotland. I'm here to take one of your patients into police custody. Christine Higgins.'

The two women looked at each other. 'She hasn't done anything,' Ruby said as they both looked at the man like he was mad.

'Protective custody.'

'Oh aye, her dad escaped today. Did you see it on the news?' Ruby asked Mary.

'Naw. Did he escape from prison?'

'From the court. The whole place was blown to smithereens but he and another bloke managed to escape. Fifteen dead, so they said. Isn't that right?'

They both looked at the man for an answer.

'Aye, that's right,' he lied, adding to their gossip. 'You could both be next. Christine's father *is* on the run and he's been spotted nearby, so we're taking her to an undisclosed location. We want to get her away as soon as possible.'

The women stood up and walked towards the dripping man. 'You got ID on you?' Ruby said.

The man showed her his warrant card.

'Okay. Sorry about the confusion,' she said. 'This way.'

'It's no problem. It's been a long day for everybody.'

'No' me, I'm just starting my shift. Eleven to nine o'clock tomorrow morning, just the way I like it. Eh, Mary?'

'What?' Mary was following behind the other two.

'I'm just saying, we like the night shift.'

'Oh aye, it beats lying on a beach in the Bahamas any day.'

Ruby laughed as thunder exploded overhead. The lights flickered for a moment. They were in the twilight mode now, the lights dimmed.

They made their way up a wide, stone staircase. 'Has this always been a home for the mentally challenged?' Barclay asked as they reached the landing.

'It belonged to a naval family a long time ago, apparently,' Ruby said.

'It's not as big as I thought it would be,' he replied, his shoes squeaking on the tiled floor as they made a right.

'It was built onto years ago, but it's still small enough so we can give the best care to our residents.' She thought she sounded like a tour guide for somebody who was interested in buying the place.

'Are the guests all sleeping?' he asked. 'I mean, if Christine should start giving us some attitude.'

'Christine won't give you any attitude. She's such a mild-mannered girl. The others won't even notice she's gone.' Ruby looked at the man as they walked along a corridor. 'Where is she being taken to?'

'Undisclosed location. The less you know, the less you'll have to lie about if her father comes here looking for her with a knife. He's a very dangerous man. If he does show up, don't put up any resistance, just call us.'

Aggy gave Ruby a look; *fuck that*. They would tell the nut bag whatever it was he wanted to know. They weren't paid enough to be heroes.

They came to the end of the corridor where Ruby stopped outside a room and Mary walked round Barclay to join her.

'We'll just make sure she's decent.' They walked into the room and Ruby tried to shut the door but Barclay had his foot in it.

'Don't be long. If Higgins is around this neighbourhood, then he won't hesitate to kill you both.'

He heard low, rapid chatter as the two women got the teenage girl out of her bed and dressed in a tracksuit. Barclay stood with his back to the door, having taken his foot away.

He heard it open wide and the two women stood with Christine Higgins.

'She doesn't say much at all. Nothing really, to be honest. Not after what happened to her and her sister. But I expect you know all about that.'

'I do. Can we hurry it up, please. I've just had a message from one of my officers that Higgins has been seen again. A tip from the public. He's not far away.'

'What if he does appear?' Ruby asked.

'Don't worry, I'm going to have two patrol officers sitting outside in a marked car. You can lock your front door and don't open it for anybody other than a police officer. Do you understand?'

Another rumble of thunder crashed above them. Ruby put a weatherproof rain jacket on Christine, who didn't put up a fight.

'Is she... will she give me any problems? In the car?' Barclay asked.

'No. She's had her meds. There's a bag there with the meds she takes with instructions on when she gets them, and how much. That sort of stuff.'

'Thank you,' he replied, putting the plastic bag in his pocket. 'Come along, Christine. You're going to be alright.'

The nursing assistants walked downstairs and stood looking out through the glass in the front door before Barclay opened it and stepped out into the pouring rain, the girl by his side. He walked to the left towards the end of the car park, then they saw two headlights come on, the beams cutting through the downpour.

When the car was driving past them, they shut the front door and bolted it. Ruby pulled a roller blind down on the back of the door.

'Let's go and finish our tea,' she said.

Mary stood looking at the door.

'What's wrong?' Ruby asked.

'What? Oh, nothing. Just a feeling I got,' she said. 'Just somebody walking over my grave.'

They drank their tea as the thunder carried on outside.

EIGHTEEN

He didn't think the rain would keep many people off the streets, especially since it was dark now, and he was right.

The ne'er-do-wells must have been in the house, drinking Buckfast, or whatever it was the wee hooligans drank nowadays.

He pulled the car into the side of the road and parked it. He had almost forgotten to put the false plates on it, but after grabbing something from the chippie, he drove somewhere secluded and changed them.

The takeaway was beyond reproach. That's what he loved about Fife; they did a really good fuck-off fish supper. The car would be reeking afterwards, but who gave a toss?

Rain was spitting on him as he walked towards the house. The street was black and dingy, the orange glow from the streetlights not worth a sook.

He had his hat on, the scarf wrapped around his face. He didn't stick out so much now, just another geezer walking home from the pub, pished. He strode up the path to the front door of the house.

He took out the key he had. The old woman inside didn't have anybody that came to visit. He knew he wouldn't be disturbed.

He went upstairs, banging his feet on the stairs. 'It's me!' he shouted.

'Oh, good. Come away upstairs, son.'

The woman's voice echoed down the stairs to him and he smiled.

She was in bed. The shabby blanket was pulled up to her chin as she sat up. The old TV was playing on one corner of the drawers and she muted it when he knocked and came into the room.

'Don't mute that for me,' he said.

'Och away. I would rather sit and have a gab with you than listen to that drivel.' She smiled at him.

'Do you mind if I use your bathroom?' he asked her.

'No, no, not at all. You know where it is.'

He heard her put the sound back on as he walked along to the bathroom. This next bit was going to shock her, but it had to be done.

He went into the bathroom and stripped his clothes off until he was naked. Then he took a drawstring bag out of his doctor's bag, opened it and pulled out a see-through poncho, the kind that tourists wore in the High Street in Edinburgh in the summer. He slipped it over himself and pulled the hood up. He pulled on a pair of nitrile gloves.

Then he took the hammer out and went into the bedroom.

He rushed at her, not giving her time to scream, before he brought the hammer down on top of her head. Once, twice, three times. Then once again for good measure.

The blood spatter was on the wall, the ceiling, the carpet and the bed covers. And his poncho.

He carried the hammer back to the bathroom where he washed it in the sink. Then he stood in the shower and let the water wash the plastic garment. He turned the water off then dried his legs and feet with a towel. Stepped out onto a bathmat and ran the towel over the poncho. When it was mostly dry, he took it off and returned it to the drawstring bag, then put it away before getting dressed. He took off the nitrile gloves, putting them in the bag, then he put on a fresh pair before leaving the house.

Back to the car.

He drove a short distance and stopped on a quiet part of the country road and took the magnetic plates off. He wondered what he would do if the police spotted him now. Then he smiled in the dark of the car.

He knew exactly what he would do.

NINETEEN

DI Ronnie Vallance pulled into the side of the road and honked his horn. He was outside one of the bungalows in Logie Green Road, down from the church. He wasn't sure if it was still a church or not, but there was a sign for some training school at the side where cars exiting from Tesco came down.

The net curtains twitched and DS Eve Bell waved to him with two fingers, telling him she was either going to be two minutes or she didn't appreciate the horn blowing.

He was listening to Forth 1. He kept the car running with the blower going and a window open. The day had started out warm with a clear sky but God knows how long that would last.

A young woman came rushing down the street and ran onto Eve's pathway. The front door opened as if by magic, and they swapped places after a few seconds of chat.

Vallance had the driver's side at the kerb, so Eve ran round to the passenger side.

'Jesus, boss, I'm so sorry. Bloody kids were messing about in the kitchen. My husband's doing the backshift just now, and he had a few tinnies last night when he came in. I told him not to, but you know how it is...'

Vallance had his pipe in his mouth, unlit. He held up a hand. 'Take a breath there, Eve, or you'll burst a lung. Don't worry about it.'

'Thanks, sir.'

'I have kids, too. The struggle is real.'

She was getting her breath under control when Vallance pulled away from the kerb.

'When did that Lidl spring up?'

The supermarket was opposite Eve's house.

'A while ago now. It's handy for getting the groceries. I mean, Tesco was too, of course, but this is right across the road.'

'Handy for letting the kids nash across.' He removed his pipe from his mouth and put it in his jacket pocket, which was no mean feat considering how big he was.

'They're only ten and seven, so maybe not quite yet,' she said as he stopped at the light.

'God, it's been a very long time since I was down here. Everything's changed. I came here when I was a laddie. There used to be a Vogue furniture warehouse there at one time. My old man brought me down to Powderhall some nights, when they had the greyhound racing. You remember that?'

He turned right into Broughton Road and headed round towards Rodney Street.

'How old do you think I am, sir? I'm a spring chicken compared to you.'

'Enough of your bloody lip. That's twice you've made me feel old in the space of five minutes.' He nodded across to some flats. 'There was a picture house there years ago. The Ritz. Of course, it was in the way of some developer who thought it was better we have some flats there instead of somewhere people can go and watch a film.'

'It's progression.' She flipped down the sun visor, opened the mirror cover, and started pouting her lips, trying to apply some lipstick without taking her eye out.

'Progression? I don't see the point of knocking everything down just to slap flats up. See what they did in South Queensferry? There was a Hewlett Packard there years ago, then some other electronics place, and guess what's there now?'

Eve managed to get the lipstick on without disembowelling herself. 'Houses,' she said, flipping the visor back up.

'Did you know that, or were you just going along with the flow of the conversation?'

'I just took an educated guess.'

'Bloody houses. Right near the train station. Dalmeny. It's become a commuter town now. There's no work there hardly, unless you have a PhD in cash registering.'

'Don't knock it. I worked behind a till for a while after I left school.'

'I'm not knocking it, Eve, but there are no prospects in that town now. Meanwhile, the fat cats are singing all the way to the bank.'

'Davie and I are thinking about buying property, did I tell you that?'

'I thought you owned your house already?' He drove round Picardy Place and up Leith Street. The new St James Centre was still being built. 'Don't even get me started on that bloody place.'

'We do own the house, but Davie's mum died last year, and left us enough money that we could buy a wee holiday home somewhere. Just a wee getaway up the Highlands or something. Davie said we should get a static caravan in Pitlochry, but I want to get something that will gain value. Know what I mean?'

'Did you see what the hotel is going to look like?' Vallance said.

'You're not even listening to me, sir.'

'I am. It just boils my blood.'

They were heading down the Bridges now.

'You never said where we're going,' she said to him as they crossed over the High Street where the throng of tourists was beginning to build.

'Niddrie.'

'Just for a wee drive, or...?'

'Boy, that lassie got your adrenalin going this morning, didn't she?'

'If you mean my babysitter, then yes, I was starting to panic. She was late, then you turned up early...

'On time.'

'...and then the kids were settling down to watch cartoons and they needed their breakfast. I swear I come to work just for a rest sometimes.'

'I hear you. My twin boys are sixteen, and if you think it's hard having one teenager in the house, try having two the same age. My daughter's married and away, so that's a blessing.' He slowed down for a bus pulling out. 'Anyway, we think we've found the motorbikes they escaped on from the courthouse.'

'All in good condition with serial numbers we can trace so we can make an arrest?'

'Burnt out. They knew what they were doing,' Vallance said.

'These things are sent to try us.'

'Do you ever miss being a cashier in Tesco?'

'Sometimes. But it was almost like being a copper at times; people shouting at you, wanting to batter you, swearing at you, even being spat on.'

'But you get a discount on a pound of mince.' He smiled at her. 'Let's not forget that.'

'Silver linings,' Eve said.

The small trading estate was off Peffermill Road, along King's Haugh. Vallance saw the forensics van and a couple of patrol cars blocking off the entrance to the warehouse they were looking for.

When he parked up, a young man in a suit walked up to him. 'DS Kennedy, Craigmillar CID, sir.'

Vallance introduced them then looked up at the roof of the warehouse, which had a big, charred hole in it.

'Run me through it, son.'

'This warehouse is split into two units. The others round about it are vacant, but available to lease. A treble nine was called by a passing van driver from one of the other units down the road. This was yesterday afternoon. Fire and Rescue attended and the flames had gotten hold of the roof by then. When they got inside, the place was empty except for the burning motorbikes. But an accelerant was used and the whole inside was engulfed.'

'Then you got a call to attend?' Vallance said.

'Yes. Myself and a DC attended as it was classified as arson by the fire commander at that point. When it was safe to go in, we saw the bikes. We were busy looking for witnesses, but to be honest, a bike being burnt out isn't an uncommon thing. So we didn't prioritise it. It was only after we read the bulletin about the escape from the court, and then the fact they escaped on motorbikes that we investigated the possibility that these could be the getaway bikes. We called forensics in.'

'Good job.' Vallance looked around. 'I don't suppose there's any working CCTV around here, but check on the other places nearby. Whoever left the bikes here, had to leave somehow. And I'm assuming they didn't walk.'

'I have uniforms doing a check right now, sir.'

'Good.'

One of the forensics team approached them. 'We found the VIN plates on the bikes. No attempt to hide or deface them. They're burnt but we can have them cleaned up.'

'They were probably all stolen, but we'll at least get an idea from where.'

He turned to Eve. 'We'll get back to the station. Not much else we can do here.'

TWENTY

'Do you think we should get a cat like Mia?' Alex asked.

'Don't get me wrong, I love cats, but they require a bowel movement depository to be cleaned with an inordinate frequency.'

'Is that a yes or a no?'

'Think litter box, and which one of us would get landed with cleaning it.' Harry sat down at their little bistro table at the window in the living room.

'I had cats growing up.'

'We had dogs. Don't get me wrong, I like both, but when you tell a dog to heel, he comes running, but when you tell a cat to do something, it looks at you and does its own thing. Like it's calling you a peasant.'

'Cats don't have to be taken out for a walk in the rain and you get a lie in at the weekend.'

'There is that advantage. But animals restrict you.'

'Maybe you're right. When we go away on holiday,

somebody would have to look after him.' She sat down beside him.

'What holiday?' he said, biting into some toast. The sun was out and it was warm already, but a few clouds scudded about with a threatening look.

'It's called a honeymoon. When we eventually get round to tying the knot.'

'I'm not averse to that—' He was interrupted by his mobile phone which spat out a tune and bounced around the table. 'Hello?'

After talking briefly, he hung up again.

'That was Ronnie Vallance. It seems our motley crew rode the bikes down to an empty warehouse in Duddingston and set fire to them. And the warehouse in the process.'

'We should get going. We can always talk about our holiday later on.'

'I'll give it some thought. I promise.'

'Just like you promised you'd get yourself a decent new car.'

'Now, now, let's not hit below the belt.'

'I should have taken the bus,' Jimmy Dunbar said as he and Robbie Evans entered the incident room.

'The traffic's nonsense through here,' Evans complained.

'If you didn't drive that jalopy of yours like a bloody clown car, we might have got here earlier.'

'How's the hotel?' Harry asked.

'Not a bad wee gaff, Harry. But greetin' face there threw a hissy fit when there was no bacon waiting for him.'

'I bet there was bacon at the Holiday Inn.'

'You know where else there's bacon? In the wee food van outside the station in the Outer Hebrides.'

'He's missing his dog, Scooby, that's why he's ornery,' Evans said, sitting down at a computer.

'Right, Harry, what have we got?' Dunbar said. They sat at a desk while the others were bustling about.

Eve Bell waved good morning to them as she tapped at a keyboard. Ronnie Vallance came over to join them.

'Morning, everybody. DS Bell· and I were at Duddingston, where six motorbikes were dumped in an empty warehouse and set on fire.'

'Do you think they could belong to the escapees?' Dunbar said.

DI Karen Shiels walked over. 'We were having a chat a few minutes ago. It's a good possibility. The usual thing for the joyriders in Niddrie is to just get off the bike and set fire to it. It doesn't make sense for them to put the bikes in a warehouse and torch it. That would bring too much heat down on them, if you'll pardon the pun.'

'What about CCTV?' Evans asked.

'We got to thinking about that yesterday. We saw the bikes shooting down the High Street then splitting off. There were six bikes waiting, ready for Higgins and his men to ride off into the sunset. So you would think, six riders, each take a passenger. But that's not what they did.'

'Were the riders wearing leathers?' Dunbar asked.

'Yes, sir.'

'How the hell did Higgins and his men have time to change into leathers and then get away on the bikes?'

'They didn't. They were decoys, meant for us to believe that's how they escaped. To throw us off the scent.'

'Was CCTV checked to see what time they arrived?' Alex said.

'Yes. They were there for two hours before everything happened. The six riders, their helmets still obscuring their faces, walked along the road and went down the News Steps. And disappeared.'

'What do you mean, disappeared?' Harry said.

'We got hold of CCTV from Waverley Bridge, and they don't come down that way. Yes, there are a lot of tourists coming and going, but no bikers. I reckon they went halfway down and changed out of their leather jackets. Maybe put their helmets in a backpack along with their jackets. There are a lot of tourists use that short cut. They would have blended in.'

'Where would they get the backpacks?' Evans asked.

'That's the mystery right there. But somebody could have been waiting halfway down with a few. That's the obvious answer.'

'You said you thought they were decoys,' Dunbar said. 'So you think they got changed and came back an hour later. That would show up on CCTV, surely? Them coming back to the bikes with their gear on.'

'It would. But the camera views from around the court don't show any bikers coming back,' Karen said. 'But this morning, I called a friend of mine who works for the *Edinburgh Evening Post* and he was there yesterday. Let me show you.'

She went to a desk and they gathered round as she started going through the photos.

'The bikes are there. Next to two police cars. But watch this.' She zoomed in closer. 'Everything starts happening. The roller door goes up and smoke pours out. Then thicker smoke. Then the van rolls out, well ablaze, and if you look just over the front of the van, there's a minibus that's been parked up. Then you see one of the bikers, then the others, all piling out of the minibus. Then all of a sudden the prison van is well alight and there's much more smoke.'

'Did you check and see how long the minibus was there?' Harry asked.

'Simon Gregg was helping me. The minibus was there for under thirty minutes. My theory is, they changed out of their biker gear as I said, then they were picked up by the minibus, driven to the court where they waited, and when it all went down, they were dressed in their leathers again then they came out and started throwing smoke grenades. Which would give Higgins and Conrad plenty of cover. Then they got back on the bikes and rode off. They were the decoys so Higgins and the others could escape.'

Harry stood looking at the photos. 'You said Conrad was seen on camera down on Market Street going into Waverley Station, but Higgins and the others weren't. There's a possibility they got in that minibus.'

'That's what I thought,' Karen said. 'I did a check, and officers were already making their way to the court-house. The minibus was stopped by a patrol at the top of St Giles and High Street.'

Everybody was looking at her like they were waiting to see who the murderer was in a soap opera.

'It belongs to the Church of Scotland. Inside were six ministers going to St Giles Cathedral. They were all wearing dog collars. So the officer just waved them on.'

'Christ,' Dunbar said. 'It would only take them a minute to put on a shirt and dog collar. Whatever the formal name for those things are. It could all have been waiting in the minibus for them and then all they'd have to do is slip it on.' He looked at Karen. 'I don't suppose they took the number down?'

'Yes, they did. The van belongs to the church, but it was only late afternoon that it was reported stolen when somebody went to use it. They didn't even know it was gone.'

'Any news on it today?'

'Not so far.'

'Damn good work, Inspector,' Dunbar said.

'Thank you, sir.'

'How many immediate family members does Higgins have living in the Glasgow area?' Harry asked.

'Just his wife and daughter. His parents are dead, and

so are his in-laws,' Dunbar said. 'We're watching other addresses.'

'And you said that your team have spoken to the wife and daughter?'

'Just the wife. The daughter, Christine, is in a care home. She was almost catatonic after the attack on her and her sister Rebecca. The lassie's a wreck by all accounts. I don't think Higgins will risk going to see her. But I'm not taking any chances. I posted a patrol car outside the home last night. I'll get my DI to personally go round there to check on things. Let me give him a call.'

He walked away to an isolated desk in the corner.

Detective Superintendent Percy Purcell came into the incident room and beckoned Harry over. He was holding a piece of paper in his hands and thrust it in Harry's direction.

It was either the list of names for the Christmas raffle or else something was up.

'This has gone tits up big time already,' Purcell said.

'What's wrong?'

'Doctor Kenneth fucking Conrad, that's what's wrong.'

Dunbar approached him, his phone call finished. 'I take it by the tone that you haven't caught him, sir.'

'Damn straight we haven't caught him. We think he's claimed his first victim already.'

'Aw, Christ. How can we be sure?'

Purcell's face was grim. 'An old woman died in her house. The doctor who came round to see her was called

Kenneth Conrad.' He looked at the two detectives. 'There's a DI on the scene this morning. Go and see him. DI Matt Keen.'

TWENTY-ONE

DI Tom Barclay pulled up behind the patrol car in the unmarked Ford. The day was grey and dismal, the remnants of the previous night's storm still lingering like a cheap aftershave.

He walked up to the passenger side, unnoticed for a few seconds as the uniform in the passenger seat was busy talking to the driver. He gave out a loud laugh before his colleague nudged him. His smile fell as he saw who it was. He wound the window down.

'Morning, sir,' he said. The heat escaped from the car, as did the smell of bacon rolls.

'Anything going on?' Barclay asked.

'Nothing exciting, sir. But we've only been here for an hour. The nightshift blokes said nothing happened during the night. They got called away but it was a false alarm.'

'What time was this?'

'Late. After eleven or something. The rain was coming down something fierce.'

'They were told not to move.'

'The caller said they thought they'd seen Higgins.'

'They didn't catch him though, did they?'

'No, sir.'

Barclay stood up straight. 'I'm here to check on the Higgins lassie. You two stop pissing about in there and keep your bloody eyes peeled.'

The men didn't answer, but Barclay thought he could hear them laughing as the window was rolled up. He couldn't blame them; there had been at least a dozen sightings of Archie Higgins since he clocked on this morning. Even his wife thought she'd seen Higgins walking down the road outside their house before breakfast. This was getting worse than Jack the Ripper. Every man and his dog swore they thought they'd spotted Higgins. God knows what would happen if they offered a reward for information.

He walked through the entrance to the home, between stone pillars standing guard. Large hedges lined the property, and inside, a lush lawn was on either side of the concrete pathway. *It's lush with all the bloody rain.*

The old mansion was in the distance. It was four storeys high, if you included the attic windows. Back in the day, one way to show your wealth was to build a huge pile and give it a fancy name. He wondered what the original owner would have thought of his home being turned into another kind of home, one that housed people with mental health problems, but who weren't a danger to themselves or others.

He climbed a set of stone steps and into the reception area, where he was met by another glass door facing him. There was a window in the wall on his left, with a door next to it.

A woman behind the desk looked up when he walked in.

'Help you?' she said.

He showed her his warrant card. 'I'm just here checking on Miss Christine Higgins. Making sure everything's okay.'

'She's fine, I'm sure. The staff know who to look for if her father shows his face round here.' She reached over for a phone and looked up at a clock on the wall. 'Ruby. Can you come to reception?'

She hung up and looked back at Barclay. A few minutes later, another door opened into the office and a woman appeared.

'Anything wrong?' the woman said, looking worried.

'No. This detective wants a word.'

'My name is Detective Inspector Tom Barclay. I'm just making sure Christine Higgins is okay. Her father is still on the loose.'

The woman stood silent for a moment before answering. 'She's not here.'

Barclay felt the adrenaline kick in. 'What do you mean she's not here?'

'I mean, she was taken out of here last night.'

'Who took her?' the receptionist asked.

'*He* did. Tom Barclay.'

Barclay stood looking at the women. Then he took his phone out.

TWENTY-TWO

'That was a first for me,' Archie Higgins said, sitting in the kitchen chair, looking out the window at the loch in the distance.

'You sure nobody knows about this place, boss?' Hugh Stern said. He had played a good part as one of the security guards, but he was a worry wart at times.

'As we've discussed before, this place is not in my name.'

It was just the two of them here. The others had all split up. Safety in numbers, except when the police had a manhunt going, then it was every man for himself.

Higgins drank some more of the coffee. He felt confident they would be safe here until he could regroup with his wife and daughter, then they would make their way to South America. Nobody would ever hear from them again.

He loved this little place, out in the middle of

nowhere. Scotland at its finest. The loch was just down the road. Some rivers too, not a stone's throw from here. It was the peace he savoured though.

It was a pity that Rebecca would never see it. There was a fantastic back garden with high hedges. A real suntrap now when the sun was high in the sky.

He felt himself choking up when he thought about his wee girl.

'Give me some peace, Hugh,' he croaked, and the big man left the kitchen, knowing the boss wanted to be alone with his thoughts.

Higgins drank more coffee and noticed his hands were shaking a bit. Rebecca. His poor, wee girl, lying in the cold ground, all alone, when she should have been celebrating life, going to university, meeting a man, having kids, making him a grandpa.

All because Eddie fucking Wise took his eye off the ball that night. He'd had explicit instructions to make sure the girls were safe, that some wee arsehole didn't try and act the big man by asking his Rebecca for more than a dance.

Of course, they weren't to know that a couple of perverts were there that night with their niece. Yes, the guest list had been checked out, and everybody's name had been given the once over, but nobody knew the stupid cow of a mother would invite the two uncles along because she had work to go to and didn't want to trust some stranger to take the girl home.

The St Charles brothers' names hadn't been on the

list, and had only been added when they had turned up with their niece.

Eddie Wise should have been all over it. Useless bastard.

He sat back and looked out of the large, kitchen window, his mind drifting back to that night...

TWENTY-THREE

'I hope this Fife guy is up to snuff,' Jimmy Dunbar said from the back seat, his preferred seat of choice when Evans was driving on unfamiliar roads. That way, he wouldn't see it coming when Evans stuck the car into an overpass at high speed. 'My hair wasn't grey until I started working with him,' he complained. 'I've had to shave it close to my heid so the grey won't show so much.'

Evans looked in the rear-view mirror and shook his head.

'He's the DI who dealt with my mother's death,' Harry said. 'He's a pretty good guy.'

'Aw sorry, pal. I didn't mean to make light of that just then. It's that heid the baw, he brings out the worst in me.'

'No bother, Jimmy.'

'I heard that,' Evans said.

'You were meant to. And stop looking in the bloody

mirror. Keep your eyes on the road. You do enough gawking in the mirror in the hotel room, I bet.'

'I take care of my hair, sir. Before I get old and wrinkly and my hair turns grey like somebody else I know.'

'Oh aye, and who's that then?'

Evans looked in the mirror. 'My old granny.'

'Aye, it bloody better be your granny. Now shut your piehole and get us across the bridge in one piece.'

Alex smiled. She wished Jimmy Dunbar and Robbie Evans were part of the Edinburgh team, but as it was, they had worked on several cases together recently.

'Where did this murder occur?' Evans asked as he floored it leaving the Queensferry Crossing bridge.

'First of all, *Captain Kirk,* slow the fucking car down. This car has six speeds and one of them isn't *warp.* Harry knows the way. And he would rather guide you from the back seat than through a fucking medium.' He looked at Alex. 'Apologies for the French, hen, but his driving does my tits in.'

'It's okay. I'm a big lassie.'

'So is Robbie. He starts greetin' at cartoons.'

'Och away and don't talk pi—'

'The next exit,' Harry said.

Evans took the main road into Dunfermline, and Alex had her phone out with Google maps open.

'Turn right, Robbie, next junction, and follow the road along. There should be patrol cars there.'

'I hope Matt Keen's there,' Dunbar said.

And he was.

118

There were two patrol cars and a decidedly better-looking pool car than the one they were in.

'DCI McNeil, good to see you again, sir.'

'You too.' He made the introductions.

'Show us this house, son,' Dunbar said.

It was a block of four houses, two doors in the middle, with one door at each end. Keen led them to the one on the far right.

'Anything come from the door-to-door?' Harry asked as they walked up the driveway, which he assumed was once all garden until pavers were laid for a car to park on.

'We have a couple of sightings of a man wearing a "funny hat". That was how it was described,' Keen said. 'A quick search with an iPad and it was correctly identified as a trilby. The man's description: dark jacket, dark trousers and medium to heavy build.'

Harry looked at Dunbar. He knew Conrad had bought a hat in Tesco.

'What about forensics, sir?' Alex asked.

'We're still going over the findings because it was only reported as a sudden death last night, and when it was deemed a homicide, the crew came out this morning. But we did recover a syringe from the rubbish bin. The householder said the doctor gave it to him but it appears that only his fingerprints are on it.'

'You think this could be a waste of our time?' Dunbar said. 'Older son, living with his mother, kills her and then blames Conrad, whose name he no doubt saw on TV.'

'We're keeping an open mind, sir. I mean, he could have seen the man in the hat walking about, just like the neighbours did, and used that figure to blame the death of his mother on.'

'Was he taken in for questioning?' Evans said.

'He was. We asked him about his mother, but he kept to the same story without deviating from it one little bit. We brought him home, because we're not going to charge him as of yet, pending further enquiry. But there was a treble nine call made from a phone box not far from here. Somebody obviously disguising their voice, said they thought their neighbour had killed his mother. Saw him injecting her with something.'

'Let me guess,' Dunbar said, 'when you asked the neighbours, nobody knew anything about a phone call.'

'Correct.'

They went through the main door into the house and entered the living room.

'What's going on?' the man said. He was sitting on the couch, and his eyes were red.

'Stanley Adamson, this is DCIs McNeil and Dunbar. They'd like to talk to you about yesterday.'

Adamson remained seated. A Family Liaison Officer came through from the kitchen. 'Tea anyone?'

They all refused the offer, except Adamson. 'I have a bladder like a camel, my mother says.' Then he looked at a space on the wall, like he saw his mother there.

'Can you tell us about this doctor?' Harry said.

'Mother wasn't due a visit. Getting an appointment for her is like winning the bloody lottery. You dial the surgery number and hope it's your lucky day. If it's not, then they give you one weeks away. Sometimes I think they hope you'll die before you can make it in. Mother wasn't due to go for another two weeks.'

'This doctor just turned up unannounced?' Dunbar asked.

Adamson looked at him, maybe searching for a hidden meaning in the question. 'Aye. She was in pain with her back. She was seventy-nine. Eighty next month. He came in, and he seemed to know what was wrong with her. Said he had something to give her. But he wanted me to go and get some chest rub. I went round to Asda.'

'How long were you gone?' Evans asked.

'Twenty minutes, tops. I might be an old fart in my fifties, but I can get a spurt on when I want. Like when I go to the local to play dominoes and time is getting on. Mother would worry about me. If I was one minute late, she'd be on the phone to the hospitals. Then God forbid, the mortuary. She even called the police one night.'

'You married?' Dunbar asked.

'No, and I fucking well resent any accusations. I do alright, you know.'

'Easy, Stanley. You don't mind if we call you Stanley, do you?' He turned to the FLO. 'Maybe we should have a cuppa. Give Stanley extra sugar in his tea. I think he's still in shock.'

'I don't take sugar in my tea.'

'You do now, Stanley.' He looked at the others. 'Maybe we should get a seat. Take the weight off.'

They looked around, each of them taking a seat, but

nobody sat next to Stanley, like he had something they didn't want to catch.

'This is a nice house you have here,' Harry said. 'Lived here long?'

'No it's not, it's shite. I only moved back in with my mother after I lost my job last year. It's not easy trying to get another one. Ageism, they call it, and it's supposed to be illegal. You try going for a job at my age, see how you get on. I have an application in with Asda. God knows I'm in there often enough, I might as well get paid to be there.'

'Anyway, Stanley,' Dunbar said, his voice still calm and reasonable. 'What's the deal on this marriage thing? Ever been hitched?'

'Christ, what's the difference? Yes, if you must know. And yes, it failed. Happy? It wasn't my fault; I had too much to drink, the barmaid was up for a bit of fun and it all got out of hand. The bitch found out, kicked me out of my house – *my* fucking house mind! – and I ended up signing it over to her. I moved in with the barmaid, until she found some other guy and she kicked me out as well. So I moved back in with my mother. Happy days.'

'Did your ex-wife have any ill-will against your mother?' Dunbar asked.

'I can see where you're going with this; ex-wife hates husband, wants more money, kills ex-mother-in-law. She's not like that. Or at least I don't think she is. But she sold my house and moved down south. I can give you her name and address and you can have one of the plod down there check her out.'

Dunbar nodded to Keen, who took out a note pad and wrote the name down. He turned and left the room to go and make an enquiry.

'You see, Stanley, where this story of yours isn't gelling is, Detective Inspector Keen spoke to the doctor's surgery and no doctor left there to come and visit your mother.'

'They would say that. They're a bunch of useless tossers. They couldn't find a gas leak with a box of matches. They just don't want a lawsuit on their hands. Can you imagine the headline; nut job doctor kills old woman in her own home. They probably kept him in a cage and only let him out when they were desperate.'

'Did you see the news about Kenneth Conrad escaping from custody?'

'What? No, I don't read the newspaper. That's just making some rich bastard even richer. I watch Jerry Springer.' He looked at Dunbar. 'Wait a minute – Kenneth Conrad? You mean, the doctor who came here yesterday?'

'The alleged doctor.'

'There *was* a doctor here. I'm telling you.' He shook his head. 'My poor old Ma. That bastard. I wish he would come here again and I'd shove the fireside poker right up his arse.'

Keen came back into the house and beckoned for Dunbar to join him out in the hallway.

Dunbar got up just as the FLO came in with the tea.

'Does the ex-wife thing check out?' Dunbar asked,

hoping the FLO had had the good sense to lace his tea with a wee dram.

'I spoke to her on the phone. She's at work and she sounded shocked to hear about the old woman, but a neighbour approached us from across the road. He has a camera on the front of his house. Some wee buggers have been breaking into cars round here, so he had it installed a few months ago. He was upset to hear about old Mrs Adamson. He checked his CCTV and bingo. Adamson wasn't lying about a doctor coming in to see his mother. He was caught on film getting out of a green car and coming into the house.'

'Does it show Adamson leaving?'

'It does. Then the doctor leaves, and Adamson comes home. The treble nine call was logged from the phone box just minutes before Adamson's call from the house here.'

'Did the camera get the plate number on the car?'

Keen shook his head. 'No. It's not the best quality. It was a dark green Land Rover.'

'Tell me we can clearly make his face out?'

'We can look at it again and I'll arrange to have copies made, but no such luck. He was wearing a hat. Just like the one Conard bought from Tesco. My grannie's old flip phone films better than the neighbour's CCTV, but small mercies.'

'Check out CCTV from around the area, see if we can get a hit on the car. I'll leave you and your team with that.'

'Will do, sir. I'll keep you in the loop.'

'It would seem that our Mr Adamson is in the clear. But stranger things have happened. I'm willing to believe him for now, but don't let him leave the country.'

Dunbar went into the living room to gather the troops.

TWENTY-FOUR

The funeral had been dismal, just like the weather in Scotland. Rain had fallen in a drizzle, but it was dry in the chapel in the crematorium. Overly warm, Archie Higgins felt, but that was probably only him. Higgins looked over at Eddie Wise, who sat opposite, ready to spring into action with the others should anybody attempt to get at the boss.

Which, of course, they didn't.

Afterwards, there was tea and sympathy at a local hotel. Higgins made all the right noises as friends and relatives offered their condolences. Higgins was polite on the outside but his mind was going a mile a minute. Later on, he was surprised he kept as calm as he did, but he had to.

For Rebecca's sake.

Two days later, when all the fuss had died down and they were in their living room, Higgins called for his men.

Five of them stood in the middle of the room. Eddie was in front, the other four behind him.

'You need us for something, boss?' Eddie had said.

'You could say that. We're going for a little trip to deal with something.'

Eddie looked puzzled for a moment. 'Sure. Anything you want.'

Higgins stood up as Candy entered the room. 'The cars are ready,' she said.

Higgins took a deep breath. 'As you all know, my daughter turned sixteen the day she died. She loved going to our house in the country. She and her sister loved going there for the weekend, to play on the swing set in the back garden, and to enjoy the fresh air. They grew up there on the weekends in summer. It's where I'd like to take Rebecca's ashes. Scatter them so she can be at a place she loved in this life.'

There was a mumbling among the men, the general consensus being that this was a good idea. They had no choice, after all. They trooped out of the house into the two Range Rovers and headed out of Glasgow.

Higgins was in the back seat with his wife, Eddie driving, with another man he'd hired, Hugh Stern in the passenger seat. The other men were following them, and Higgins was giving Eddie directions as he went. There was never any suspicion about why he hadn't put the address into the satnav. These things had memory that could be retrieved by law enforcement.

Maybe it was an hour, maybe it was two hours. It could have been two days for all Higgins knew, because he sat in the back, playing images of his little girl in his head. The dead one. The second child, the one who had survived, was still in hospital.

Tears rolled down his cheeks and he felt his wife's hand slip into his, although he didn't acknowledge it. The car slipped through the night darkness like a spectre through a haunted wood, which Higgins thought appropriate.

The headlight beams cut along the dark road until Candy told Eddie where to turn. It seemed Higgins had given up on the directions. This road was narrower with dense brush and tree branches hanging over the lane, like they'd entered into a whole new world.

The road was windy, and Higgins turned briefly to make sure the other car was still following. Once again, a direction was given to take another road, this one even more narrow. The big SUV took it with ease and eventually they came to a driveway. It was long and winding, with more trees sheltering them from the road. The trees stepped back from the drive as they got close to the house and an automatic light came on as the headlights lit the front of the house.

Eddie sat looking at the house for a moment, waiting for Higgins to tell him what to do, or to hear the click of the door opening.

The door it was.

Higgins stepped into the cold air as the engine remained on, the lights helping to illuminate the way to the front door, despite the security light being on.

'Get the bags from the car,' Higgins ordered Stern,

who was already getting out as Higgins made his way round to let his wife out.

'This place is so special,' Candy said in a low voice. The headlights from the car behind lit them up for a second until the driver turned the main beams off.

The other men jumped out after the car was turned off. All the bags were in the front car.

'This place *is* special,' Higgins answered after a few seconds. 'It always will be.' He looked up at the house, which was large, but not one of those gigantic castles where the owner's money had been spent on every whim.

'Let's get inside,' Higgins said to Eddie, who helped carry their bags, while the other men took their own.

Inside, the place was clean. He'd made sure a cleaning company had been in to make it spotless.

'Get the kettle on, Eddie,' Higgins said, 'while we get the bags upstairs.'

'Sure, boss.'

'We'll make plans in the morning to scatter Rebecca's ashes.'

Eddie left the room and went through to the kitchen. A few minutes later he came back and found the others standing facing him. There was a tension in the air now, compounded by Archie Higgins holding a sawn-off shot-gun, pointed towards him.

'What's going on, boss?' Eddie asked.

Higgins sighed heavily. 'I wish it hadn't turned out this way, Eddie. You've been a good man for many years, but that night at the party, you were in charge of security. That meant looking after my little girls.' His breath was coming faster now, his face reddening. His eyes were wide and his mouth became a snarl.

'Listen, boss, I was right there—'

'That's the thing; you fucking weren't there! Now one of my little girls is dead and the other one is in a care home and God knows how long she'll be there. She can't even speak to me!' He raised the shotgun higher.

Eddie put his hands up and looked at the other men in the room. His colleagues. Men he trusted. And Candy. She couldn't even look him in the eye.

'Boss, I'll do whatever I can to make things right. Just give me a chance.'

'Chance? You had a fucking chance back then but you blew it. Now it's time for your punishment.'

'Aw, come on, Archie! That wasn't my fault!'

'Of course it was!' Higgins stepped forward with the gun and for a second, Eddie thought he was going to pull the trigger. 'We're going for a little drive,' he said instead.

'Aw, wait a minute. I'm not going for any fucking drive—' he started to say, but Higgins had his men rush Eddie and they overpowered him. In a couple of minutes, his hands and feet were tied.

He was struggling as he was brought to his feet and Higgins rammed the shotgun into his guts. 'Stop fucking dancing around or I'll start by blowing your kneecaps off, then you won't be able to walk.'

'Why? You're just going to kill me!'

'I'll make you die slowly, that's why. And then you'll be begging me to kill you.' He turned to Stern. 'Gag him.'

With the gag in his mouth, Eddie was thrown into the

rear of the front Range Rover, forced into a foetal position so they could get the back closed. Then they took off in both cars.

The cars bumped along the dirt road for what seemed like an eternity.

'You're sure nobody comes up here?' Candy asked from the back seat. Higgins was up front with one of his other men.

'It's private, Candy. This is our road. It leads into the woods. The cottage is a former hunting lodge.'

'It's hardly a cottage,' she replied, looking out of the wide window into the darkness.

After a little while, the car stopped. She didn't know how long they had been driving, her thoughts occupying her mind.

Higgins got out of the car, the lights at the back of the car illuminating the ground in a mix of red and white. He opened the split boot, the bottom half lying flat. He reached in and dragged Eddie out, dumping him on the ground, listening as he grunted.

The headlights from the car behind illuminated the scene like some macabre tableau. A man lying on the ground trussed up like a turkey, another man standing over him, taking a shotgun from someone else.

'You're not going to shoot him here like an animal,' Candy said, putting a hand on her husband's arm.

'I will if I want.'

Candy stepped up to him. 'No, you're not. I want to kill him.'

Her husband looked at her, madness dancing in his eyes. 'What?'

She moved inches closer. 'I said, I want to shoot the bastard. He let my little girl die and I want to finish him off.'

'This is not the kind of business you deal with.'

'I'll have somebody with me and he'll be in the grave you had dug earlier. He'll be six feet down in the ground. Let me do it, Archie.'

He looked like the curtain of madness was going to drop completely until he snapped out of it.

'Take him. It's just over the brow of the hill. You can't miss it. Hugh will go with you.'

'Okay.' She gently took the gun from him and nodded to the two men who had driven in the other car. 'Stay with my husband. You're in charge of his safety. Do you understand?'

'Yes, ma'am.'

Higgins turned to Stern. 'Go with my wife and that scumbag.'

'Yes, sir.' Stern grabbed hold of Eddie and manhandled him along the dirt track, through the headlight beams, taking him over the hill to where he faced certain death. He shone a torch in front of them but said nothing. Candy followed with the gun and her own torch.

The woods were pitch black and Candy shivered. It was cold but it wasn't the temperature that bothered her. She was still consumed by her grief. She told them where to step into the brush.

There was no footpath leading into the woods but some of the foliage had been trampled. This was it.

They came to another clearing. The torch illuminated the grave that had been dug, the mound of earth piled next to the dark hole.

'Untie him,' Candy ordered. She levelled the shotgun at Eddie and he stood still as Stern untied the ropes and threw them into the grave. It was six feet down. They had toiled over two days to dig it, Higgins had told her, making sure no animal would get a sniff of the buried corpse.

Stern stood back, his beam shining on Eddie. Then he moved some bushes aside and brought out three LED lanterns. They weren't huge but would give enough light to fill the grave in.

Eddie took the gag off and threw it into the grave before smiling. 'So, now what are you going to do?' He held his arms wide and walked towards her, slowly.

'I'm going to blow your fucking head off. Piece of shit.'

'Why?'

'Are you mental? Why do you think? You let my daughter die.'

'Stop where you are!' Stern shouted at him, but Eddie ignored the warning.

It was cold now, and Candy wished she had put on a thicker jacket. She was shivering, the shotgun wavering in the poor light.

'Candy!' they heard Higgins shout, probably alerted by Stern shouting. It was all the hesitation Eddie needed. He stepped forward, snatching the gun from Candy, pushing her roughly. She fell back into the foliage with a grunt.

Eddie heard the footsteps of Stern rushing at him, so he turned, and Stern was closer than he thought. He brought the gun barrel round in an arc, the end of the wooden stock catching Stern in the face.

It was enough to knock Stern off his feet. He looked round and Candy was lying on the ground.

He turned back to Stern and aimed the gun at him. Stern put up a hand as if that would block the buckshot that would take his head off. Instead, Eddie kicked him hard on the leg. Stern let out a yelp of pain as Eddie turned and started running along the pathway.

Stern was up and after him but two shots from the gun sent him scattering into the bushes where he fell and rolled down an embankment.

When he stood up in the dark, he couldn't hear or see Eddie.

He was gone.

Higgins heard two shotgun blasts echo through the forest and he sucked in a breath. It was over.

He wanted to run, to see if his wife was okay, but he was sure she would be, and if he disturbed her, she would be furious with him.

'Let's give it a couple of minutes,' he said to the two men who were with him.

Then they saw the lantern lighting her up as she came walking over the hill, Stern limping behind her.

'I'm sorry,' Candy said.

'Don't be. The bastard deserved it.'

'No, I mean...' She started sobbing.

'He got away,' Stern said, and that's when Higgins saw the blood on Stern's face.

'I want to sit down,' Candy said, her eyes looking glazed.

'What the fuck happened?' Higgins said as his body-guard opened the door for her. She sat in the back of the Range Rover with the heat on.

'He approached Mrs Higgins,' Stern said, 'and I thought she was going to let him have it, but he overpowered her. I tried to tackle him but he belted me with the gun. He kicked me and ran off. I went after him but he shot at me. I'm sorry, boss.'

'Never mind that bastard. I'll have a contract taken out on him. Get my wife home and we'll get her cleaned up.'

'Right away, sir.'

They all got in the cars and went back to the house.

Archie Higgins drank more coffee. He thought about Eddie Wise, about him dropping off the face of the planet. Higgins pictured Eddie lying dead in a grave. Those were the thoughts that got him through the day.

But the thoughts only served to dredge up memories of his dead daughter.

Higgins got up and went through to the living room. He switched on the TV. Even the TV licence had the real owner's name on it. He sat down in one of the over-stuffed chairs and picked up the remote from a little side table. He idly flipped through the stations but nothing caught his attention.

Nothing on TV remotely came close to the drama that was going on in real life.

He heard the car come back. Hugh Stern returning from calling Candy. He stood up and walked to the front door, opening it.

Stern came walking in like a tornado.

'What's up, Hugh?' Higgins asked, startled. He wasn't a man who startled easily.

'I couldn't get through to Candy. Her phone went to voicemail. So I called one of the team back in Glasgow. He made discreet enquiries and called me back at the phone box.'

'Get to the fucking point, Hugh.'

'Candy's gone. She was abducted last night. And not only her; Christine was taken from the home.'

TWENTY-FIVE

Jimmy Dunbar heard the news before Archie Higgins. He sat in the unmarked car, talking to DI Tom Barclay.

'Apparently, I went into the home last night and took Archie Higgins' daughter. I took her into protective custody.'

'Tom, for fuck's sake, you been on the hooligan juice again? And this early? I don't want to come down heavy-handed, but if you've been on the bottle again, I'll kick your tadger round the back of your heid.'

'Naw, sir, I haven't touched a drop. That's what the folks in the home are saying. Somebody walked in, showed them a warrant card, introduced himself as DI Tom Barclay, and waltzed out with the wee lassie, Christine.'

There was silence in the car for a moment.

'Sir? You still there?'

'I am indeed, Tom. We're being played around with by Archie Higgins, and I don't like it one little bit. He obviously knows me and members of my team, and now he's taking the piss.'

'You think that Higgins is behind this?'

'Don't you, Tom?'

'I'm not so sure. It was a hell of a risk to take, sending somebody in there to get his daughter. But that's not all, sir.'

'Christ, what else?'

'Candy Higgins is gone, too.'

'How in the name of fuck did that happen?'

'There was a storm last night. I think the patrol took their eyes off the ball.'

'Off the ball, Tom? They better not take their eyes of their own fucking balls by the time I'm finished with them. But how do you know it was an abduction?'

'There was some blood on the carpet. It looked like there had been a tussle. A lamp knocked over, some stuff in disarray.'

'Christ, maybe somebody's out to get Higgins, if he wasn't the one responsible. Let's look at both angles there. And get back to me soon. I want regular updates.'

'Will do, sir.'

Dunbar got out of the car and walked back up the path to Adamson's house.

'Somebody abducted Archie Higgins' wife, Candy, last night,' he said. 'And somebody masquerading as my DI went to the home where Christine Higgins lives, and abducted her too.'

'How could somebody just go into the home and take her?' Harry asked.

'He had a warrant card in the name of my DI, Tom Barclay. When Barclay went to the home this morning, to check on her, she was gone. The night staff told him somebody using his name took her. He had to get another member of the team to go there to confirm who he was. The staff thought he was at it.'

'I was assuming that Higgins' wife and daughter would try to meet up with him,' Alex said. 'Nothing like this.'

'What makes it an abduction though?' Evans said. 'It could just be staged to make it look like an abduction, since Higgins is obviously desperate to have his family back together.'

'It seems that was the clever way to get her out,' Alex said.

'That would have been the obvious answer, Robbie, if it hadn't been for the blood on his wife's living room carpet. It's not a blood bath, but enough to suggest that she was struck and was bleeding. Higgins wouldn't have wanted to have his wife hurt.'

'Unless he was staging this as an abduction,' Harry said.

'You don't know Higgins, Harry. His family was everything. He wouldn't hurt Candy, not after what happened to his daughter, Rebecca.'

'Who would want to take Higgins' wife and daughter? I'm sure there are plenty who would want to take over his businesses.'

Dunbar shook his head. 'They're mostly gone. His

wife sold them off. There's nothing left of the Higgins'
empire to speak of.'

'Somebody's pissed off at him, that's for sure, though
it's only to be expected. But maybe if we can find him,
then we'll find his family.' Harry looked at Dunbar for a
moment. 'Don't take this the wrong way, but do you think
it's possible...?'

'That Barclay really did go in there and take the
Higgins girl? No. He was in the incident room with five
other people at the time. I did wonder the same thing
myself, Harry, that's why I made the phone call checking
up on him.'

'That's a relief.'

'Did you talk to your own DI?'

'I did. She had the others do some background on
Kenneth Conrad. His family came from Fife, but when
he was a little boy, his parents were killed in a car crash
and he was put into care.'

'How long was he there for?' Dunbar asked.

'Until the age of eighteen. He was there for five years.
He left the foster mother's care and moved.'

'Are his foster parents still around?'

'The mother is. And get this; she lives in Ballingry.
Not that far from Lochgelly,' Harry said. 'It's not that far
from here,' Harry said.

'Let's go.'

TWENTY-SIX

DI Tom Barclay walked into the doctor's surgery and immediately felt like he was going to vomit. It was the smell. Always the smell. Not as bad as a hospital, but this was a close second. The antiseptic smell, which in turn conjured up the vision of a needle. And not any old needle, a huge fucking thing that would pierce his whole body, not just his skin.

'...you?'

He blinked a couple of times and looked at the woman behind reception. 'Sorry?'

'Can I help you? Do you have an appointment?'

'No. But I need to speak to the head doctor, or whatever his title is.'

'She. Dr Angela Cummins. Can ask what it's about?'

'No.'

The woman looked at him. She was no doubt used to fending off irate patients, people who were sick and waiting to see the doctor, who was invariably running late, leaving them to read some tatty old magazine that Barclay thought of as germ farms.

'It's important,' he said, feeling himself sweat. Didn't they open any windows in here? No wonder people got sick.

'I'll see if she's available.' She held his gaze for a moment, and was about to lift the telephone receiver when a woman walked past on the way to the waiting area.

'Oh, doctor,' she said. The woman turned round.

'Yes?'

'This is a detective who would like a word with you.' She said it with a tone that suggested that if the doctor couldn't manage it, then she wouldn't lose any sleep over it.

'DI Tom Barclay,' he said, introducing himself. 'It's important that I talk with you, doctor,' Barclay said.

She hesitated for a second, then relented. 'Follow me.'

Barclay complied, half-expecting her to snap on some disposable gloves, but she merely walked down the hallway into her office.

He sat down opposite her.

'This hasn't been easy for this practice,' she said before he had a chance to speak. 'I knew you'd be round here eventually. Bloody Kenneth Conrad. He almost put us out of business. There's only two of the original staff still here. We're lucky we have any patients willing to come here after what he did.'

Her cheeks were getting flushed but she relented and let Barclay speak.

'Do you know if he's made contact with anybody here at the practice? Or any patients that you know about?'

'I think most of the elderly patients have barricaded themselves in.' She sat forward at her desk. 'But no, nobody's said anything about him contacting them.'

'Would any of the previous doctors tell you if he contacted them, or they thought they had seen him?' Barclay said.

'The term, *clutching at straws* springs to mind, Inspector.'

'It's not as uncommon as you think.'

'Probably.' She thought for a second. 'There was one phone call yesterday. From the doctor who Conrad worked with when he was here, a locum; Michael Salamin.'

'He called here?'

'Yes. He was naturally worried. He has every right to be. He thinks that Conrad will come after him.'

'Do you have his details?'

'No. He moved down to London and changed his name legally. Mud sticks, sometimes.'

'What, did he think that Conrad was going to go to the trouble of tracking him down?'

'He didn't say, but he was full of questions. He seems very worried but I reassured him that Conrad would be in leg irons before the sun goes down. Isn't that right?'

'We're working on it, Dr Cummins.'

'Any luck?'

'We're following up some serious lines of enquiry.'

'You've got hee-haw, as my father would say. Conrad's in the wind, and as far as we know, he could very well be on the Caledonian sleeper to London to chop up Doctor...'

'Doctor...?'

'Christ, it didn't occur to me to ask him what his new name is now.'

'I'm sure he's taking adequate precautions. Besides, we think that if Conrad can disappear, then he might get up to his old ways again.'

'Might be hard for him to play the part of doctor, don't you think? His face all over the news, and no doctor's bag to bluff his way into a house with?'

Barclay nodded. 'Maybe you have a point.' He reached into a pocket, took out a business card and put it on her desk. 'Thanks for your time. If you get any more calls, or anything else to do with Conrad—'

'I'll call you.' Angela Cummins picked up the card and looked at it for a second. 'Just don't hold your breath. Kenneth Conrad is probably long gone.'

TWENTY-SEVEN

Harry sat in the back of the pool car with Dunbar, while their two sergeants sat up front, Evans behind the wheel again.

He'd told Evans he wanted to start by going through to Lochgelly, and Alex gave him directions.

'Alex was brought up in Dunfermline,' Harry explained. 'She knows her way around here.'

Alex instructed Evans to take the A92 off the M90, and there was an exit for Lochgelly.

'I've never been in this part of the world,' Dunbar said.

'I know it like the back of my hand,' Alex said. 'I dated a guy from around here.'

'We don't want to hear any graphic details of your former conquests, sergeant,' Harry said.

'Merely pointing out I know the lay of the land.'

'Was that his reputation?'

'You're too funny, sir. I hope you bear that in mind later when we're alone.'

'Just concentrate on the job in hand,' Harry said.

They took the appropriately-named Station Road and soon they were upon Lochgelly station. Evans pulled into the little car park on the right-hand side, which sloped upwards and they got out.

The road ran under the station's platforms, heading north to south. At the top of the incline, wind blew across the fields, negating the warmth from the sun overhead.

'I want to see where he would have come down,' Harry said. 'It would be the other side if he was going to make his way to Ballingry before he went to Dunfermline.'

'Which we're assuming he would do because he needed transport,' Harry said.

They got back into the car. Evans turned right and slowed as he came out from under the short tunnel. Steps leading down from the platform led to the pavement at street level. Evans put the hazards on as they sat in the car.

'So, he would have come down here, and if we suspect he was heading for his old foster mother's house, he would have headed north, up that way, away from the tunnel,' Harry said, pointing.

'How far is Ballingry from here?' Dunbar asked.

'It's about five miles, I think,' Alex replied. 'Not far by car, but it would mean he was out in the open if he was walking.'

Harry saw a bus stop on the opposite side. 'Let's head into Ballingry.'

Evans started the car and after they'd driven a short distance heading north, they saw the bus stop.

'He could have risked getting the bus, but a lot of them have cameras on them nowadays,' Dunbar said.

'We can check with the local bus depot. Meantime, let's get to the address of Conrad's foster mother.'

The drive took minutes, and Alex had Google Maps up on her phone, giving directions, until they were driving along Ballingry Road, heading east. They saw the bus terminus on their left. Opposite was a walkway that led into a street, along from the street that they were looking for.

'Turn right,' Alex said, and they all started looking for house numbers.

They found the house at the bottom of the street. They were terraced houses, and the end one had its door on the end of the building, isolating it from the neighbours.

They got out. The air was warm but had an unpleasant odour.

'Looks like a tip,' Dunbar said, nodding to the detritus behind the scraggy hedge. A badly kept garden wall continued from the hedge and there was another little garden, filled with litter that had been blown into a heap by the wind.

'How old is this woman?' Evans asked.

'Late seventies,' Alex answered as Harry walked up to the front door.

He peered through the letterbox after ringing the bell. He couldn't hear any movement from inside.

'She's been poorly,' a voice said from the street.

They all turned to look at the older woman.

'I'm sorry?' Dunbar said.

'Mrs Peacock. The lady who lives there. She's been poorly for months now, and I've been looking after her. I was going to be bringing her something to eat shortly. She has the appetite of a hen.'

'You have a key to get in?' Harry asked. 'We're police officers.'

Like they'd been rehearsing for this very moment, they all brought their warrant cards out.

'I do. I also clean for her. Poor thing, she's frail now. Too proud to ask me for help, but I come in with some dinner, to make sure she eats,' the woman said, walking up the pathway and bringing the key from her pocket.

'I'll take that, if you don't mind,' Harry said.

The woman looked like she was about to argue then handed the key over.

'Try and be quiet. Mrs Peacock likes to rest during the day. Personally, I think she has the c-word.'

Harry immediately discounted the clap and erred on the side of caution. 'Cancer?'

The woman looked around as if the disease had manifested itself into a walking beast and was coming down the street right now.

'Aye. Early stages. That's why I'm helping her. Lung cancer, it is. Not that the useless twat of a doctor could tell the difference between lung cancer and a boil on her arse. *It's just a cough, Mrs Peacock*, he said. Cough my Aunt Fanny. That cough was the first step in her getting the lid screwed down. But I'm no doctor.'

'Doctors are under a lot of pressure,' Dunbar said.

She rounded on him. 'I'm no' sayin' anything different, pal. But unless you hunt them down, they don't bother coming. I still go in every day but I haven't been in today.'

Harry had the key in the lock and the door was open before the woman could say any more.

The hallway was dull and smelled of something Harry and Dunbar were both familiar with. 'Bedrooms upstairs?' he said, turning round. Alex was behind him. 'Ask the neighbour,' he said to her.

'Bedrooms upstairs?' she asked and got a nod in return. Dunbar and Evans came in behind them.

The stairway was on the right and Harry led the charge, although this charge was one step at a time, testing each step like it was going to crack and break.

'Somebody else clear the house,' he said from the first stair.

Evans and Alex said they would. The neighbour was about to help when Harry put up a hand.

'Please stay outside.'

She looked miffed and took her mobile phone out. Either warning the killer upstairs or getting the war drums going.

'You smell that, Jimmy?'

'I can hardly miss it,' Dunbar replied.

They made it to the landing upstairs. Four doors. All shut.

'Slow and methodical or—' Harry started to say when Dunbar booted the first door. It clattered back on its hinges, revealing an avocado green bathroom that the eighties were missing.

'It's empty then?' Harry said.

Dunbar nodded. 'Get that one open sharpish, Harry. If Conrad is in here, he's going to get a belting before we do.'

They took their batons out. 'If Mrs Peacock has a cat, there won't be room to swing it, this house is so small,' he said, putting weight on the handle of the next door. He leant on it and pushed the door in as hard as he could, raising his baton.

The dead woman wasn't going to rush them. Not with her skull smashed in.

'Fuck this,' Dunbar said, and booted the next door. That room was empty. So was the next one.

'There's nothing in those other rooms,' he said. 'No furniture, nothing.'

'Is everything alright up there?' Alex shouted. Evans was already on the stairs, then Alex followed.

'We thought the old boys were in trouble,' Evans said, grinning.

'Enough of your bloody lip. There's a murdered woman in there,' Dunbar said.

'How can you tell she's been murdered?'

Dunbar stood to one side.

'Oh, right. Shit. Conrad?'

'I would say so. He's obviously pissed off at people he knew,' Harry said. 'Plus, she's an old woman and we know the thing he has for old women,' Harry said.

'Call it in, Robbie,' Dunbar said.

TWENTY-EIGHT

Forensics turned up after the circus arrived in town, which consisted of what was probably the whole of the Lochgelly police station and an ambulance. And a superintendent.

'We've got the town on lockdown,' the super said. 'If he's still here, he won't get out.'

Harry thought the bluster was for their benefit, as well as to have witnesses that he had done everything possible, should there be an enquiry in the future.

'I doubt he's still here,' Dunbar said.

'What makes you say that?'

'As far as we know, Conrad only has one connection to this town, and she's lying dead upstairs.'

'If he's right,' said a suited SOCO, coming to the front door, 'then he'll be miles away. That woman's been dead for around twelve hours. That's my guess, but the pathologist will nail it down. I'm just going by what I've seen at crime scenes.'

The super nodded, his grim face telling them he thought his pension was more than hanging in the balance. The weasels would be here from the daily rags soon, all of them throwing mud and not caring where it stuck.

'Why do you think this Conrad bloke didn't go back to Glasgow?' the super said. 'If he has money and he's resourceful, then he could be anywhere.'

'We're covering all the known places he was associated with in Glasgow. He can't go anywhere near his old haunts. He might very well go back there eventually, but he's not stupid. At the very least, he'll wait until the heat is off a bit then make a move.'

'Then where would he go?'

Dunbar looked at the man; tall and skinny with a thin moustache. And not an ounce of gumption.

If we knew that, we'd be arresting him. 'That's what we're trying to figure out, sir.'

'Is there any chance he might not have done this?'

'There's always that chance, but it would be a hell of a coincidence,' Harry said. 'Do you know where the doctor's surgery is in Ballingry?'

'There isn't one. It's in Lochgelly.' He gave Harry directions.

'I saw a doctor leave last night. Didn't get a good look at him though 'cause it was pissing down and blowing a gale. It was like one of those farmer's green Land Rovers.'

The team walked down to their car. 'Alex, get onto the surgery, see what info you can get on the doctor who came here to see Mrs Peacock.'

Alex nodded and walked away. The sun went behind a cloud for a moment, making the breeze seem chilly.

'Get your team onto Conrad's background,' Dunbar said. 'They're doing a good job but we need to find out if there are other people connected to him.'

Harry turned to the neighbour, who by now had rustled up some friends for the show. Harry took his phone out and opened the photos app.

'Have you seen this man?' he asked the neighbour, showing her a photo of Kenneth Conrad.

'That's the bloke from the TV. Naw, I haven't seen him around here.' She turned to the gaggle of women who all agreed that their nosy network would have seen him if he'd shown his ugly mug round here.

'It's not to say he wasn't here,' he said to Dunbar.

'Tell us more about this doctor you saw,' Evans said.

'I didn't speak to him. I just saw him from my window. He came out of her house and walked round the corner, then he was gone. But he was wearing a funny hat and a scarf round his face.'

'How do you know he was a doctor?'

'He was carrying one of those doctor's bags. Do you think he did something to her?'

'It's possible. Give my sergeant a description of this doctor,' Dunbar said.

'You hear that, Betty,' she said, turning to the rest of the gossip committee. 'It's possible, he says. My God, he might have had his way with me if I'd gone in.'

'I don't think you would have had anything to worry about,' Betty replied.

'Cheeky cow.'

Evans took out a notebook and started taking down a description. When he was finished, he approached Dunbar. 'Average height, average build. Wearing the hat and scarf, like she already said.'

'Just add a yellow hard hat and it's Bob the bloody Builder,' Harry said.

'Conrad bought a hat just like the one being described,' Dunbar said.

'What would Conrad have to gain from killing his old foster mother?' Evans asked.

'He had power over her. Sometimes that's all they need, I suppose,' Alex answered. 'There has to be a connection between her and the victim we just saw in Dunfermline.'

'Lochgelly said none of their doctors have been here to see Mrs Peacock. Whoever was seen coming out of her house, wasn't a local doctor. It had to have been Conrad.'

TWENTY-NINE

'It's all over the bloody news already,' Commander Jeni Bridge said, pointing the remote at the TV in the incident room and wishing it was a hand gun. She pressed a button and killed the picture.

'There's been no sighting of the car,' Harry said.

'Why in God's name would he kill his foster mother?'

'As far as the neighbours knew, he hadn't seen her in years. He didn't visit very often. He moved to Glasgow when he was eighteen.'

'It's possible he just wanted to steal her car,' Evans said.

Dunbar threw him a look. 'I don't think so. He could have got a car anywhere. Maybe he wasn't up on the ins and outs of how to nick a motor, but he was taking a hell of a risk turning up there. I mean, what if we knew about her sooner than we did, then we could have been waiting.'

'There's just one fly in the ointment with that theory;

the neighbours all look out for each other there and it's a small town. They would have seen him coming, unless he waited for darkness, but when he got off the train, it was still light with hours of daylight left.'

'What about the victim's own family?' Jeni asked.

Dunbar shook his head. 'Husband died years ago. No offspring of her own. She took in foster kids. Most of them without any future, and she kept them to adulthood.'

'Maybe we're looking at the wrong picture here,' Harry said. 'Hear me out; Conrad killed elderly patients because they were easy targets, and by all accounts from his psychiatric reports, he couldn't help himself. The Crown didn't want to know, of course, and he got life in Barlinnie, but then he had an opportunity to run, so he's on the lam. He has these feelings inside, and he needs to take care of the urge to kill. Giving grandmas and grandpas an overdose of morphine isn't an option now, but killing them with blunt head trauma is. And one easy target was his former foster mother.'

'Somebody dropped the fucking ball on this one. I mean the team who put this together. Even the lone gunman had to come from somewhere.'

Harry tapped the whiteboard with a pen, hitting a photo of Conrad. 'Who else would be an easy target?' He turned and faced the other detectives.

'People he knew in the foster home,' Dunbar said.

'Right. And can we find out where they are?'

'Already on it, ma'am,' Gregg said. 'Social services will know, but their offices are closed right now.'

She rounded on him like he'd just insulted her. 'Get somebody to get back in there and find the information for us.' She turned back to Harry and Dunbar. 'He's well ahead of us, and I won't be surprised if he's already killed again.'

Half an hour confirmed that nobody would be in to check the records until the next morning. The snooty man on the phone said their social workers were busy with *real* work, looking after people who needed them, and that they were stretched like an elastic band as it was. He would make sure that somebody got the note first thing in the morning.

'Let's hope nobody on that list dies tonight,' Harry said.

THIRTY

'You look like somebody stole your ball,' Alex said, hanging up the phone. The pizza was ordered and would be delivered in fifteen minutes.

'What?' Harry looked round at her. He'd been gazing over at the bowling club but his mind was a million miles away.

'There's been sightings of an alien in Inverleith park.'

He looked at her blankly. 'I'm sorry, I wasn't listening.'

'I know I'm not the best detective on the force, but yes, I worked that one out.' She smiled and sat on the couch. 'This case getting to you?'

'Hmm? No. I mean, yes, it's frustrating, but that's not what's on my mind.'

'Want to share?'

He looked at her as if he was chewing it over, but then the coin toss landed on the side of divulging. 'I'm worried about Chance.'

'I know what you mean.'

'Do you?'

'Harry, my love, I've seen kids battered by so-called loving parents. The people who those kids have to trust. I know Chance is seventeen, but he's still a boy. I'm worried about him. Is he still with your brother?'

'No. Derek called me earlier and said Chance went back home. He hasn't spoken to him today.'

'Have you tried calling Chance?'

Harry nodded. 'I have. It goes to voicemail. So does his mother's. I can't get hold of him.'

Just then, the doorbell rang. 'That'll be our guests,' Alex said, getting up from the couch. She opened the front door. It was Chance.

'Oh, hi!' she said. 'Come on in.'

'Hi, Dad,' Chance said when he walked into the living room.

'Hi, son. Everything okay? He didn't touch you again, did he?'

'No, no, nothing like that. I was wanting to have a talk with you and Alex.'

Harry briefly looked over at Alex who just smiled at him. 'I'll get an extra plate.'

'Oh, I'm not disturbing you, am I?'

'No, you're fine. Our colleagues from Glasgow are coming over for pizza. You can join us. It will be here shortly.'

'Are you sure? I can come back...'

'Sit down, son.'

A few minutes later, Alex let in Jimmy Dunbar and Robbie Evans.

'Gentlemen, this is my son, Chance,' Harry said, making the introductions. 'He dropped by.'

'Good to meet you, son,' Dunbar said, shaking hands. Evans did likewise.

Then the pizza arrived and they sat down round the little bistro table. The five of them, crammed in.

'I wanted to have a talk with you, Dad, that's why I came round, and it's even better that you have two other detectives with you.'

They were all silent, looking at him.

'I want to join the force.'

Harry looked shocked for a second before replying. 'That's terrific. What does your mother think of it?'

'She doesn't know. She would blow a stack. And Tam, well, he's not exactly on the side of the law. He said he would kick your head in if you ever tried to interfere with him and Mum.'

Harry took a deep breath to calm himself.

'Who is this guy Tam?' Dunbar asked.

'My ex-wife's new boyfriend. He's been getting rough-handed with my boy, Jimmy.'

'Has he now?' He glanced at Evans and a slight look passed between them. 'He's not family, is he? If he's only her boyfriend?'

'No, he's just another in a line of men she brings home,' Chance said. 'I was going to have it out with him one night, but Mum stopped me. She said he would kill me. And maybe she's right, but I want to make myself better. I want to join up and work my way up like you guys.'

'That's very noble, Chance,' Evans said. 'Don't let anybody put you off.'

'That's the thing, Robbie, Tam would go nuts. He's not the most squeaky clean guy I've ever known. There's no way he would let me in the house knowing I wanted to be a cop.'

Alex made a face and reached to put her hand on his. 'Why don't you come and live with us, sweetheart? We have a spare room.' She looked over at Harry, her eyes starting to get glossy.

'I couldn't do that. You and Dad are just starting out together, Alex. I couldn't impose. I'll put my dream on hold for a while. I just wanted to know what you thought of my plan, in case I can make it happen in the future.'

'Oh, honey, you're not imposing, I promise you. What about it, Harry?'

'You did say you wanted to hear the pitter-patter of a child's feet.'

She made a face and squeezed Chance's hand harder. 'That's it settled; you can stay here.'

'I'll need to drive home and get my stuff. If you're both sure.' He looked at them each in turn.

'We're both sure,' Alex said.

'Thank you. You don't know what this means to me.'

'I'll drive you over when we're done with the pizza,' Harry said.

Again, the look between Dunbar and Robbie Evans.

'No, Harry, let me and Robbie drive Chance home. Where is it you stay, son?'

'Kelty, in Fife.'

'Right, then. You keep us right, and we'll take you there. You can tell your mother your plans, and we'll help you get your stuff. We've already been to Fife today, so we have an idea where we're going.'

Chance looked at Harry.

'That's fine, son, if DCI Dunbar doesn't mind.'

'Ach, it's no problem. Call me Jimmy.'

'Thanks, Jimmy,' Chance said.

'One thing before we hit the road; Robbie and I have been talking music, so let me have your opinion on this, Harry; *Always on my Mind*. Elvis or the Pet Shop Boys?'

Harry thought about it for a moment. 'Pet Shop Boys.'

'What? Away, man.'

'I liked *West End Girls* too.'

'You're dead to me.' He stood up from the table. 'Right, Robbie, get over the road and bring that piece of scrap you call a car over.'

'You can take my Audi if you like,' Alex said.

Dunbar held up a hand. 'Thank you, but no. Robbie's going to have to learn, if he wants to wench a young lassie the proper way, he'll have to fork out for a decent motor. Not that tin Lizzie he's driving.'

'Ach, away and gie yersel peace. That car's a classic.'

'Maybe in fifty years' time. Right now, it's a piece of scrap metal on wheels. But go and get it anyway.'

THIRTY-ONE

Candy was shivering in the dark. It was summertime but it was freezing. There were no windows in this room, only a door.

Christine stirred by her side. Her daughter hadn't uttered a word while they had been here, which wasn't a surprise; the girl hadn't uttered a thing since that night.

The night her sister had been murdered.

She heard the key turning in the lock and the door opened. He came in and smiled. Took out a phone.

'This is a burner, so it can't be traced. I'm going to send a photo. He'll get the message.'

She held onto her daughter, a frightened look on her face as he held the cheap phone out in front of himself.

He took several photos, then put the phone away.

Candy smiled and stood up.

'Come on, Christine. Let's go and get something to eat.'

The man led them upstairs where it was warmer.

'I'll have the rooms made up. You'll be safe.'

'I don't know what I'd do without you,' she said.

He put a hand on her shoulder. 'That's what friends are for.'

THIRTY-TWO

After they hit the Queensferry Crossing bridge, Chance told Evans it was a straight drive up the motorway.

'Right,' Dunbar said, 'how about *I Fought the Law*? Bobby Fuller Four or The Clash?'

'The Clash,' both Chance and Evans said at the same time. Evans, despite driving, put a fist between the seats and Chance fist-bumped him.

'Pair of heathens.' Dunbar turned to look round at Chance. 'And I'm going to tell your bloody faither what you're like.'

Another ten minutes and they had taken the slip road off the M90, and turned right into Kelty.

'We're in your hands from here on in, pal,' Evans said, as Chance told him to turn left at the next junction and then guided them to Centre Street.

His mother's flat was in a little cul-de-sac with half a dozen houses in it.

'It's up there,' Chance said. 'Hers is the upper flat.

The front door is on the side. The one nearest the back, I mean,' he said, pointing to the two main doors. 'The other one is for the old boy who lives downstairs from my mum.'

Chance opened the back door, got out of the car and stood looking at the four in a block.

'We'll come in with you, son,' Dunbar said, and his tone suggested that it wasn't an option.

The sun had fallen away now, leaving dusk to encroach and take over. It was cooler in the shade and Dunbar could see the boy was shaking.

They crossed the road and walked along the path at the side of the house, past the neighbour's door, and when they were almost at Chance's flat, his front door swung open violently.

'Where the fuck you been?' a man said, his voice full of menace. The door was reached by climbing a couple of steps, so it wasn't easy for him to take a step out towards Chance, which Dunbar thought might have happened if it had been level with the path.

'Yeah, where you been?' his mother said from behind the man. 'Out my way, Tam.'

Morag McNeil had let herself go, Dunbar was sure, when he saw the woman; greying hair swept back into a ponytail, wearing a polo shirt that any charity shop worth its salt would have binned, and shell suit trousers that might have been in fashion thirty years ago. Maybe the same charity shop should have set fire to the shell suit.

'And he's brought the fuckin polis wi' him. Hope yer proud of yersel, boy,' Tam said, poking his head back round the door jamb, eyeing up the suits. 'What's he fuckin' done?'

'You do know my dad's in the polis,' Chance said.

'None o' yer bloody lip. I told you what would happen if you brought the filth round to my doorstep.'

Dunbar took a step forward. 'We're friends of his old man, nothing more. Chance isn't in trouble.'

'Just as fuckin well.'

'I'm going to stay with my dad,' Chance said. 'I'm just here to pick up some stuff.'

'What did you say?' Morag spat the words out.

'I'm going to stay with my dad.'

'No, you're not. You're staying right here.'

'I can go if I want. I'm seventeen.' Chance barged past his mother and Tam and thumped up the stairs into the main level. They turned and followed him and Dunbar made his way in, Evans right on his heel.

The décor shouted out *corpie chic* with its embossed wallpaper and cheap carpet with its gaudy flower pattern.

'Who invited you in?' Tam said, blocking their way in the lobby.

'I did,' Chance said, poking his head out from a bedroom on the right. The kitchen was on the left, from where came the smell of fish and chips. 'Get out of their way.'

'I'd listen to him, Tam, if I were you,' Dunbar said.

Tam was about to protest when Morag shouted through from the living room straight ahead.

'Tam! Chance can't leave. He's staying right here.'

Dunbar and Evans walked into Chance's bedroom, watching while he speed-packed, like he was on a game show and the clock was ticking. It was a typical boy's room, with posters on the wall, and a couple of model airplanes sitting on a dresser, but they were from bygone days, when the boy was younger.

'Get that fuckin stuff unpacked, ye wee scrote,' Tam said. His belly was straining against his string vest and he brought himself up to his full height. He took a step into the room.

'Who's going to stop me?' Chance looked at him.

'I will. Just like the last fuckin' time.'

'You're not going to be doing anything, sunshine,' Dunbar said.

'You think some old, skinny weedgie bastard like you is going to stop me? Cop or no cop, I'll batter the living daylights out of you and your fuckin' wee boyfriend, just before I teach that ungrateful wee fucker a lesson he'll never forget.'

He had started to bring a knife out from his pocket but Robbie Evans had turned and took a step closer, headbutting the big man hard.

Tam's nose broke and blood gushed out as he fell backwards, landing outside the door in the hallway.

He looked shocked for a moment before raising his head. 'Ya wee fanny.' He was looking at Dunbar. 'You need that wee twat to fight for you? He your fuckin boyfriend or something?'

'Deary me, what kind of talk is that?' Dunbar turned to Chance. 'Look away. Keep packing.'

'I saw nothing.'

Dunbar took a step forward and stepped on Tam's groin, not quite putting his whole weight on the man's balls. 'I'm going to say this, and you're going to listen without interrupting. You hear me?'

Tam's eyes were wide and he nodded quickly.

'This wee fanny and his boyfriend are going to drive Chance back to Edinburgh, where he's going to live with his old man. You're not going to object, or make his life hard. Are you?'

Tam shook his head.

Dunbar put more weight on Tam's nether regions. Tam squealed a bit.

'If I hear one word that you've been giving this young lad a hard time, I'll have some friends of mine drive through from Glasgow and have a wee chat with you. They won't be members of Her Majesty's Constabulary, but they're still friends of mine.' Keeping his foot where it was, Dunbar leaned down closer. 'And I promise you one thing; you'll never see it coming.'

He stood up straight and put a little bit more weight down. 'Do you understand?'

Tam nodded and made a sound like an animal.

'You're going to wish young Chance the best of luck from now on, because you're never going to see him again. Neither is his mother, unless he chooses to see her.'

Tam locked eyes with Dunbar.

'Well, go on then, Christ, what you waiting for? Your balls to pop?'

'Best of... luck, Chance. Nice knowing you... son.'

'There,' Evans said, 'that wasn't so bad.' He stared down at Tam.

'No. No, it wasn't.'

'Tam!' Morag shouted through. 'What's going on? You giving that pair a belting?'

'Shut up, Morag. Everything's fine. I've decided that maybe... it's better to let Chance go.'

'Why are you talking funny?'

'Shut up, woman. I'm having a moment with the boy.'

Dunbar removed his foot. 'Remember what I said. Me standing on your bawbag will be a picnic compared to what my friends will do. Think *vice* and *mincer* and that's not their names.'

'Are you sure you're coppers?' Tam asked, his breath coming in gasps.

'No more questions.' Dunbar turned to Chance, who had a holdall and a small suitcase packed.

'You ready, pal?'

'I am.'

'Right, get your fat arse out of the fucking doorway,' Dunbar said, and Tam scrambled backwards until they could get round him.

'I'm away, Mum. Don't call me. I'll call you. Maybe.'

Morag stood in the living room doorway, smoking a cigarette. 'You go and live with that useless bastard of a father and you need never come back here again. Don't bother calling me.'

Chance shrugged and carried his bags down the stairs.

JOHN CARSON

'Why are you lying there?' she spat at Tam. 'And what's that on your face?'

'I fell, ya stupid cow. Open your fuckin een. It's blood.'

'Useless arsehole,' Morag said. She turned back into the living room and slammed the door shut.

The two detectives stood with Chance down at the car.

'You okay?' Dunbar said to him.

'I'm fine. I couldn't have gotten away without your help. Thank you.'

'Don't mention it. Put your bags in the boot.'

Chance didn't look back as the car drove back along Centre Street, heading towards the motorway.

'Skinny? Cheeky bastard,' Dunbar said as they hit the slip road. 'I prefer to think of it as looking after myself. What do you think, Robbie?'

Evans made a face. 'Why you asking me? It's not like I take notice.'

'Slim. That's how I would put it. Skinny indeed. Now, *Red Red Wine* by Neil Diamond or UB40?'

THIRTY-THREE

Harry was standing looking out the window at the bowling club, holding a cup of coffee in one hand. The sun was out; it was going to be a good day, weather wise, but he felt on edge.

'I hope they're thoughts about me,' Alex said, coming into the living room.

'As always,' he said, turning round to face her.

She could see he was far from happy. 'You're not having second thoughts about Chance coming to stay with us, are you?' she said, lowering her voice.

'What? No, of course not. I just know what a vindictive bitch his mother is. I hope she doesn't start any of her nonsense.'

Alex walked up to him and put her arms round him. 'If she does, she's got us to deal with. As I said last night, he's going to be my stepson, and a copper to boot! We'll look after him, don't worry. Robbie told me before they left last night, that he doesn't expect Tam to give Chance any more aggro. I didn't question him.'

'Then I assume Jimmy took care of things. I can relax now.'

She kissed him then let go and went into the kitchen to make coffee.

'Does Chance drink coffee?' she shouted through. 'I forgot to ask him.'

'He already out. He started jogging a couple of months ago. He wants to get into a gym and take care of himself before applying for the force. There's a stringent fitness test they have to pass to get through.'

'Maybe you should go jogging,' she said, coming back into the room.

'Do I look like a man who exercises?'

'I want you to be fit for when we eventually have a honeymoon night.' She held up a hand. 'I know you haven't asked me yet, but a girl can dream.'

'We have such an unconventional relationship; we meet at work, you rent my spare room, seduce me...'

'Tell you how I fell in love with you.'

'...then we buy this flat that I rented from Frank Miller. And us getting rings is the next step.'

'I never said I was normal,' Alex said.

'That wouldn't have been a good opening line.'

'I wasn't about to play my hand at that time.'

'Clearly.'

There was a knock at the living room door.

'Come in,' Harry said.

'Sorry to disturb you,' Chance said, dripping with sweat. 'I just got back from jogging and I know you're used to having the flat to yourselves so I didn't want to disturb anything.'

'We're hardly teenagers like you,' Harry said.

'I just need a towel. I was going to shower, but I won't be long.'

'Hall cupboard,' Alex said, smiling. 'Take your time. Your dad's going to make us some breakfast.'

'No he's not. Harry is going to usher Alex along to get ready for work. We still have two fugitives to track down. And may I remind you that we have two colleagues to meet over at the hotel?'

'Yes, sir.'

'Is he always this bossy to you, Alex?' Chance said.

'He's only putting on a show for you, Chance. I'm the boss in this relationship.'

He grinned and left to go shower.

Half an hour later, Alex was ready for work, and Chance was showered and dressed.

'Can you give me some pointers with my application, Dad?' Chance said.

'Of course. I'm sure Alex will want to chip in.'

'Of course I will,' Alex said. She was already starting to feel like a mother towards Harry's boy.

'Thanks. I promise I won't be a bother, living here. I want to get as much studying in for my application to the force as I can, then if all goes well, I could be away training.'

'You're no bother.'

Harry and Alex sat at the bistro table and Chance pulled up another chair.

'You think you would want to become a detective like us?' Harry said.

Chance smiled. 'Yes. That would be terrific. I mean, like now; you're hunting down those guys who escaped from court. That's exciting.'

'Detective work is ninety per cent paperwork with only ten per cent getting off your backside,' Harry said.

'I know, but when something like this does go down, it's exciting. I think I'd like to work my way up.'

Harry drank some coffee. 'You know, son, you're going to have to go through this process on your own. I can't put in a word for you. That's the way it is. If you get in, it will be through your own hard work and determination.'

Chance nodded. 'I know, Dad. I wouldn't have it any other way.'

'You have a good head on your shoulders,' Alex added. 'You'll be fine. They will be lucky to have you.'

'Will you want to join Edinburgh?' Harry asked.

'Where else would he join?' Alex asked.

'Not Fife, I wouldn't think.'

Chance held up a hand. 'I was talking to Jimmy and Robbie in the car last night on the way here, and Glasgow sounds like a good beat.'

Harry was silent for a moment. 'If that's what you want, I won't stand in your way.'

'I appreciate that. But I had a look at the file you had emailed to you, about the case.'

'What did you make of it?'

'To be honest, I didn't find Conrad very imposing,' Chance said.

'Imposing? He killed over a hundred of his patients.'

'Allegedly. That was supposition. They think he killed what, four women? That was the official charge, but they reckon he killed all those other old folks just because he treated them and then they died. They couldn't prove anything.'

Alex nodded. 'That was brought up in court to make sure he was put away for life. It worked.'

'I agree,' Chance said. 'He needed to be locked up for the rest of his life, but the one thing that got him nailed was having the old woman leave her house to him in her will.'

'Correct.'

'His defence was, he went out with the old woman's daughter, just to help her back into the swing of going out socially again. Then he helped her by going online and guiding her through the process of finding a friend.'

'Go on,' Harry said.

'The woman in question, Edwina Adams, said that Conrad got very familiar with her when he was round, but he denied being anything more than a family doctor, and helping her navigate her way round the internet.'

'Okay, so what does that prove?'

'Doesn't it make you wonder why Conrad would be so stupid in getting the old woman to sign over her house? If he really is unhinged, then why would he risk putting his killing spree to an end? He's obviously very intelligent, and he likes killing, according to the charges, so why would he risk it all?'

Harry drank more coffee. 'Sometimes, they think they are so far above the law, that they don't see that sort of thing as a risk.'

There was silence in the room for a moment. 'You don't believe that, do you?' Chance said. 'If I was working this case, I would go back and talk to that woman, Edwina Adams, just to get a feel for the situation.'

'Maybe we could ask Jimmy to have his DI go and have a word with her,' Alex said.

'Why not? It wouldn't do any harm.' Harry finished his coffee. 'We should be going. We don't want to be late.'

'We can talk about the case tonight, yes?' Chance said with enthusiasm.

'We can.'

'Great. I'm going to study.'

Outside in the sunshine, Harry stopped and looked at Alex. 'What do you think?'

'I think your son is going to go higher in the force than you are. He's a bright lad. I just hope he has better taste in cars.'

THIRTY-FOUR

'You two sleep okay?' Harry asked as he and Alex got into the back of Evans's car.

'I slept like a log. Cathy showed me Scooby nashing about the house, and as long as I know he's being taken care of, I'm fine.'

'What about you, Robbie?' Alex asked.

'Naw, Cathy didn't show me Scooby. I had to settle for looking at a human being. I'm just glad I'm not sleeping in the same room as him. I looked through the peephole when I got woken up in the middle of the night and saw old creepy drawers walking along the hallway in his jammies. Nearly put me off my full Scottish breakfast this morning.'

'Will you stop talking pish?' Dunbar said. 'How's young Chance this morning?' he asked Harry as Evans pulled away from the bowling club.

'Great, thanks to you two. He's even talking about going to Glasgow, if he gets in.'

'What do you mean, *if he gets in*?'

'I told him I can't pull any strings for him, Jimmy. It wouldn't look right. He has to get in on his own merit.'

'*You* might not pull any strings,' Dunbar said in a low voice, looking out the window.

'Sorry, I never heard that.'

'And let's keep it that way, mucker.'

'Tell him what Chance thinks about Edwina Adams,' Alex said from the back seat next to Harry.

'Chance reckons that something isn't quite right with the Adams daughter. He thinks that it's strange that Conrad would jeopardise himself by getting the old woman to sign over her house.'

'That did occur to me when me and the lad there were chewin' the fat on the way over from Govan. But who knows what's going through a nutter's mind when he's on the rampage?'

'Chance says if he were a detective, then he would interview the woman again.'

Dunbar nodded and turned to look at Harry. 'I can give Tom Barclay a bell and get him to go talk to her. Here, let me call him now. And you keep your eyes on the road, Robbie. I bet you didn't get any sleep because you were Insta chattin' wi' that lassie all night.'

'Are you ever going to pull yourself into the twenty-first century? Besides, she broke up with me.'

'Already? That was quick. They usually wait for a fish supper back at your place and realise what a clarty bastard you are. And by that, I mean, you don't knock the Hoover about before they get there.'

'Very funny. Just because you're an—'

Dunbar held up a finger to silence him as his phone was answered. 'Tom? It's me, Dunbar. See that old spinster that Conrad had his eye on, the one by the golf club? Go and have a chat with her again, just to get a feel for her. See if she sounds genuine.'

After listening to the reply, he hung up. 'Why can't you show subordination like him?'

'What would be the fun in that?' Evans replied.

DI Tom Barclay never had seen the point in golf. He'd never even had the remotest inclination for taking up the game, but he had to admit, it wouldn't be half bad living across the road from a golf course. Like this fancy one in Bearsden.

He stood at the front door, and hesitated for a moment. He was standing on the same spot that Kenneth Conrad had stood, when he had thoughts of murder going through his head. Barclay wondered what the doctor had felt at the time. Anxiety, in case he got caught? An adrenaline rush that no amount of illicit drugs could replicate? Nonchalance? Or maybe the sound of his neighbour's dog talking to him?

He raised his hand to ring the bell when the door swung open. He tensed, his eyes searching his would-be assailant, looking for a part of the body that would come towards him, his brain going into automatic mode to fight back.

'Can I help you?' the woman said. If he'd been an intruder, she didn't seem fazed in the slightest. She was young, looked in shape, and probably did kick-boxing practice before breakfast. She was dressed in dark trousers and a white blouse.

'DI Tom Barclay, Govan station,' he said, showing her the warrant card he'd been holding in his right hand.

'Carol Lonsdale. Here to arrest me?' she said with a smile, and for the first time, Barclay noticed the mug in her left hand.

'I just need a word with Edwina Adams,' he said, no sign of humour in his voice, which was understandable since his heart was about to go into fibrillation.

'Better come in, Inspector. Don't want the nosy sods around here gossiping.' Barclay stepped over the threshold and entered a cool hallway. 'Especially since Jack the Ripper came here and tore an old woman apart.'

'You know all about what went on in here, then?' Barclay replied, a hint of sarcasm tinging his voice.

'Well, he hardly killed them with a chainsaw now, did he? But it was bad enough. Let's go into the living room. I'm on time for work, but I don't want to end up being late.'

'This won't take long. Is Edwina Adams still here?' He knew the answer before she replied. He sat down on the settee, a plush leather affair that probably cost more than he earned in a month.

'No. I don't know her. I know she lived here, but that's only because she was in the paper. Her mother was one of the victims of the killer doctor.'

'I'm assuming you bought the house from them? Edwina Adams and her sister?'

Carol looked puzzled. 'Me and my husband bought this place, what, fourteen months ago? After all the legal wrangling. One of the neighbours told me Conrad got the old woman to sign the house over to her. But it didn't matter; he could have got Santa Claus to sign the house over. It wasn't theirs to sell.'

Barclay sat forward. 'What do you mean?'

Carol smiled. 'Don't tell me you lot didn't know? Conrad conned the old woman, but the will was as good as toilet paper. They only rented the house. It was a company that owned it. We got a good deal on it. The estate agent said the company wanted rid of it because it drew too much attention to them. So they off-loaded it.'

'Do you remember the name of the company who sold it?'

Carol thought for a moment. 'Stewart Properties, I think.'

'Never heard of them,' Barclay said, but then he wasn't in the market to either buy or rent an upmarket gaff next to a golf course.

'Neither had I, but that was the name on the deeds when we signed it. And a rep from the company was there.'

'Do you remember his name?'

'*Her*. No, but her signature is on the deeds.'

'Do you have a copy handy?'

Carol shook her head. 'It's in the bank safety deposit box.'

'Any chance we could have a look at it? Soon?' Barclay said.

'I'll nip into the bank on my lunch break.'

'I'd appreciate that.'

'Considering I own the business, nobody's going to give me a rollicking for being late.'

Barclay took a business card out and passed it over to her. 'If you could give me a call as soon as possible.'

'I'll get right on it.'

THIRTY-FIVE

The incident room was stuffy. Somebody opened a window to let fresh air in, but it didn't do much good. It had been a long day of following useless leads and it carried on into the afternoon, making them more frustrated with each passing minute.

Jimmy Dunbar was sitting at the front of the room near the whiteboard.

'I had a call from my DI back in Govan. He went to interview the woman who was essential in bringing Kenneth Conrad to justice. She doesn't live there anymore. The thing that brought Conrad down, as you all know, was the fact that he persuaded her mother to sign over the house to him. But this is where it gets strange; they didn't even own the house.'

'Did the mother have dementia or something?' Simon Gregg asked. 'Maybe she was confused and didn't realise what she was doing?'

'Not that we know of. She had cancer, and although she was elderly, it seems that she was of sound mind.'

'The daughter, Edwina Adams, is in her late forties, also of sound mind, but she's the one who reported to police that Conrad had conned her mother,' Evans said.

'Could it be that Edwina *thought* her mother owned the property?' Alex asked.

'That would mean both her and her sister were duped. It's something we're working on. But Conrad denied ever having seen such a will. He knew nothing about it, but it was signed in front of a witness, apparently. It was a DIY thing, not drawn up by a solicitor.'

'Who was the witness?' Evans asked.

'We're trying to track the paperwork down now. It was obviously presented in court, but we'll have to get the PF's office in Glasgow to give us a copy. We're also waiting to get a look at whoever signed the paperwork for selling the house.'

Eve Bell came over and handed Harry a few pieces of paper. 'I called the social services first thing and they sent this over. All the kids Mrs Peacock ever had. I marked the ones near Kenneth Conrad.'

'Thanks, Eve.'

Harry quickly scanned the highlighted names before passing the papers over to Dunbar. 'Anything jump out at you?'

Dunbar read the names and looked at the others. 'Michael Salamin was also a foster kid of Mrs Peacock's. The doctor who worked with Kenneth Conrad.'

'They knew each other when they were kids, Conrad

being the older one, but not by much. Conrad went on to become a doctor and Salamin did too,' Harry said.

'DI Barclay said Salamin left Glasgow and went to live in London and he changed his name.'

Harry turned to Eve Bell. 'Can you try and find out what his new name is?'

'Yes, sir.'

'Can somebody do a check on Stewart Properties?' Dunbar asked. Simon Gregg said he would do it.

'It's the people who owned the Adams' house in Bearsden,' Dunbar explained.

Harry looked at Eve Bell who was a wizard on the computer. A few minutes later, she came back with the answer. 'Stewart Properties are based in Fife. Dunfermline to be exact. A quick check at Companies House says that it was owned by Sir Malcolm Stewart.'

'Was?' Dunbar said.

'He died and left the company to his daughter, Candace Stewart.'

'Oh Christ.'

'What's wrong?' Harry asked.

'Candace Stewart,' Dunbar said.

'You know her?'

'We all know her, Harry. She's now known as Candy Higgins.'

THIRTY-SIX

They didn't drive north in Evans's scrapper. 'I don't feel like going into the front of a bus at high speed,' Dunbar had said, so they took a pool car.

'Shouldn't we be taking backup?' Evans said, thrashing the car like it was a Hertz rental.

'Listen, son, we're going on a sort of recce. There's a fine line between going in gung ho and making an arse of ourselves, and having a poke around. If we find out that Higgins is at this lodge, then we stay back and call it in. If he's not, we were following a lead that didn't pan out.'

'I was just thinking, if we do get there and we're spotted, then Higgins will probably be armed. And he's not going to be there by himself, let's face it. Maybe we should err on the side of caution.'

'Harry and I talked about it, and that's what we've decided. We only brought you along so you could drive.'

'Yeah, that's why. Nothing to do with the fact that Alex and I are younger and fitter and can climb fences and run fast.' He looked at Harry in the rear-view mirror. 'No offence, sir.'

'None taken,' Harry replied.

'Shut your hole and keep your eyes on the road. Bloody running. Who wants to run at my age? Why have a dog and bark yourself?'

'He's like this when he's pished and needs a drive home from the pub.'

'Works both ways, son. I remember pouring you into a fast black on more than one occasion.'

'Fair dos then.'

'But never mind your lack of driving skills. *Mad World*, Tears for Fears or Gary Jules?'

Evans looked across at Alex who was in the passenger seat. 'I feel this is entrapment. But I'm going to say Gary Jules. What about you, Alex?'

'Definitely.'

'Tears for Fears are one of the best bands from the eighties. Pair of heathens. What about you, Harry?'

'Oh, I'm not sure to be honest.'

'You're wasting your time asking my boyfriend,' Alex said. 'He still has a Jimmy Shand collection.'

'Nothing wrong with Jimmy.' Dunbar looked out through the windscreen from the back seat. 'My granddad used to play him when we went and visited.' He sat quiet for a few moments. 'Christ, now I've gone and got the *Bluebell Polka* stuck in mah heid.'

'I could think of worse things. Like that rap nonsense,' Harry said. He fist-bumped Dunbar.

Evans looked in the mirror again. 'Rearrange these two words into a well-known phrase; *duddies* and *fuddy*.'

'I'll give you fuddy duddies. Better than going to a nightclub where you have to learn sign language just to chat to a woman, the music's that bloody loud. Am I right, Harry?'

'You are that, pal.'

'Cathy and I have been at many a ceilidh.'

'His dug's feared when he comes in blootered wearing his kilt. He thinks there's a bad man in the hoose.'

Dunbar ignored him. 'See, when you two finally tie the knot, you should wear a kilt, Harry.'

'I already explained to Alex that I was wearing a kilt first time around when I got hitched to Morag.'

'So? Who gives a toss? It wasn't you wearing a kilt that messed up your marriage, was it? Or did a sudden breeze blow your kilt up and she saw what she was going to get on her honeymoon night and thought she'd been short-changed?'

Alex and Evans laughed.

'I don't know what you're laughing at,' Dunbar said to Alex, 'it's your turn next.'

'I can assure you no gust of wind made my wife faint.' Harry looked away out the window, as he felt his face starting to burn.

'There you go then. That lassie is marrying a true Scotsman. If she wants you in a kilt, make her day.' He leaned forward and slapped Evans on the back of the head.

'What was that for?' Evans said.

'To stop the next thing you were going to say from coming out of your mouth.'

Dunbar's phone rang and he took it out of his pocket. Spoke to the caller before hanging up. 'That was my DI. The woman who owns that house forgot to go to the bank at lunchtime to look at the deeds, but she left work early. She looked at the signature of the person who sold the house: Candace Stewart.'

'Using her maiden name,' Harry said.

'Which she may use for business purposes. It's not illegal.'

They approached the village of St Fillans, at the east end of Loch Earn.

'I wonder if the Mirror Man is in the water,' Alex said.

'What's that?' Evans said.

'It's a sculpture of a man made out of mirror tiles.'

Nobody knew whether the man would be there or not.

'The small road is on the right as we're leaving the other end of the village,' Dunbar said.

They approached the Four Seasons hotel on the right, opposite the loch itself. Then Evans saw the road, right after the hotel.

He turned into it, immediately swinging a left into a smaller road with a canopy of trees hanging over it.

'There's a couple of houses then the lodge is at the top,' Dunbar said. 'We'll park near it and walk the rest of the way.'

THIRTY-SEVEN

'I'm going mental here,' Archie Higgins said. 'Where the bloody hell can Candy be?'

Hugh Stern was looking out the window again, drinking coffee, acting like they had nothing better to do than prepare to go for a hike. Higgins wished he'd remembered to bring his golf clubs with him so he could bend one over Stern's head.

'How should I know?' His tone was becoming more belligerent by the hour. 'He sent you a photo and he'll be in touch.'

'This is not helping. This place is too isolated. We should have gone to Glasgow, not come up here. I mean, what was Candy's old man thinking, buying this place?'

Stern turned from the window to look at Higgins. 'That was his business. Maybe he wasn't a whiney baby like you. Maybe he liked the idea of going to the golf club along the road, or nipping down to the hotel for a few swifties on a Saturday night with his missus. You know, normal stuff that people do at the weekend. Not thinking about taking somebody's tadger off with a screwdriver.'

'You fucking listen here...' Higgins started to say, but there was something about Stern's smile that sent a chill through him. Higgins had been in many a fight, but there was something wrong with Stern, maybe a couple of wires in his brain that weren't quite making a connection. Higgins didn't want to rub him the wrong way, especially since it was just the two of them here.

He turned away and went through to the kitchen. Maybe a cup of coffee would help him think. Maybe if he threw it at Stern and smashed the mug in his face, it would make him feel good again.

Somehow, he couldn't see Stern lying down and taking it. When this was over, Stern was on his own, Higgins thought as he poured boiling water into a mug and added instant coffee. Maybe he, Higgins, would arrange for an accident to happen. Nobody would miss the brain dead prick.

The house phone rang and Higgins almost dropped the kettle. 'Who the fuck is that?' he shouted through to the living room.

'Sorry, I seem to have forgotten to bring my crystal ball. And my powers of telepathy seem to be on the blink,' Stern said.

'You'll be on the fucking blink in a minute.'

'What?'

'Just answer the bloody phone, will you?'

Brilliant. Just bloody brilliant. Higgins had asked Stern to use the public phone in the village so that there would be no trace of them using this one, and now some-body was calling. It couldn't be a double-glazing sales-man. It had to be something regarding his wife.

'Hello?' Stern said after answering, like he was talking to a scammer, but actually about to give the man his bank details. No rush, no suspicion in his voice, just a good old get-together with the Prince of Nigeria.

Higgins walked into the room and Stern turned away from him, like a lassie who'd just been caught by her father, talking to the local hoodlum.

Stern picked up a pad that had been sitting by the phone, and a pen, and wrote something down.

'Right. Okay, I understand. You'd better be there,' Higgins heard Stern say. There was a garbled reply. 'Oh, I'd like to see you fucking try. Just be there.'

Stern slammed the phone down and Higgins' heart leapt.

'Who was that?'

'Candy's abductor.'

'What? Have you never fucking watched TV before? The negotiator never speaks to the nutter like that! What if he takes offence and kills her? For fuck's sake.'

'He told me that if I messed him about, then he'd kick my head in. Me? Cheeky bastard. I'll rip his fucking face off. Talk to me like that.'

'Do you not grasp the seriousness of this? Some nut job is holding my wife and daughter and all you can think of is comparing willy sizes. Fucking magic, that is.' He stood and shook his head while Stern just stared at him.

'Have you finished your wee tantrum?' Stern asked.

'What is this? You never would have spoken to me like that before.'

'That was then, this is now. Deal with it.'

'Fucking deal with it?' I'll deal with *you* in a minute. He didn't voice the add-on.

'Do you want to know where your wife is or not?'

'Of course I do. Stupid sod.'

Stern thrust the pad out. Higgins read what was written on it. 'What's that?'

'That's the fucking address where they're being held.' He made a face and tossed the pad onto the table. 'There's just one thing.'

'What's that?'

'He wants you to go alone.'

'What?' Higgins said. 'It sounded like you were going.'

'No. He said if I came along, he'd make sure I die. He wants you alone.'

'Christ. What if there's a gang of them?'

'Don't worry, I'm coming. I wouldn't miss this for the world. I'm not having him talk to me like that.'

'What do you think he'll do when he sees you?'

'He's not going to see me.'

'How do you know?' Higgins asked.

'Trust me.'

That's just the thing, Higgins thought, I don't trust you one little bit anymore.

THIRTY-EIGHT

It was still light out, but the canopy of trees made it look darker. The bushes were thick on either side. They passed by a house, with nobody in sight.

'It's further up the hill, according to what I could find on Google,' Dunbar said.

'What's that, sir?' Evans said. 'You using technology? I am impressed.'

'Just keep a look out for it. We'll have cover as it's off the beaten track a bit. It's set back in its own grounds. We can approach without giving our hand away.'

'Trespass, you mean,' Harry said.

'It's all in the interpretation, Harry.'

They traipsed further up the hill then heard the roar of a car's engine. A big car by the sound of it.

They ducked into the high bushes by the side of the road and watched as a Range Rover came towards them then went speeding past without slowing down.

'You see the guy driving?' Dunbar said.

'No,' Harry said.

'His name is Hugh Stern. He works for Higgins. Come on, it's not much further.'

They got back out onto the road and a couple of hundred yards further along, they saw the entrance to the lodge house. They continued along the track leading up to the house itself.

'I don't think there's any need for stealth,' Harry said as he saw the front door wide open. They ran towards it, careful in case they were walking into a trap, but Harry felt they were going to find the place empty.

They took out their batons. 'Robbie, nash back down and bring the car up,' Dunbar said.

Evans took off without another word.

The other three moved into the house, watching each other's backs. Alex said she would check the kitchen. Harry said he would check the other rooms with Dunbar.

The downstairs was empty. They checked the rooms upstairs. Again, empty.

When they came back down, Alex was standing in the living room, holding a pad with a nitrile glove she'd taken out of her pocket.

'I think I know where they're going.'

THIRTY-NINE

There was a high stone wall opposite the little road they needed to drive down. Stern pulled the Range Rover into the side where the tiny lane opened up just for the inter-section. Higgins was lying down on the back seat.

'We're close,' Stern said. 'Swap places with me.'

'What?'

'Jesus, do I have to explain everything to you? Get your arse in the driver's seat and I'll get in there. When we're down there a bit, slow down and I'll get out. He's expecting you, not me.'

They quickly changed places. Higgins shivered. The sun was low, hiding behind the tall trees. This was a huge property with trees everywhere, but one of the attractions was the gardens, open to the public, but fortunately, they were closed for the day.

Higgins drove down the other road, passing a pond on his left. Further down, the road was no more than a paved track, and they passed a couple of detached houses.

'Turn the headlights off,' Stern ordered.

Further down, they came to a fork in the road, and they could see the old castle keep poking up in the distance. A high hedge bordered the road.

Higgins slowed down and took the left fork.

'Stop,' Stern said.

Higgins jammed the brakes on. 'What's wrong?'

'I'm going to get out and make my way through the gardens by the furthest entrance. I'll wait until it's a bit darker then I'll meet you in the keep.'

'Christ, what if he's killed us all by then?'

'You worry too much. It's going to be darker in five minutes. He won't be looking for me to come through the gardens. He's wanting you, not me. Just get going. They're probably looking for us now.'

He'd made sure the interior lights were off so the inside of the big car remained in darkness as he opened the back door and slipped out.

Higgins drove away, heading for the keep.

FORTY

'It's always like being on a roller coaster when he's driving,' Dunbar said, as Robbie Evans got his foot down.

'Scream if you want to go faster,' Evans said, unfazed.

They followed the A85 back the way they'd come, until they reached Comrie, where the speed was drastically reduced going through the village.

They turned a sharp bend.

'Next right,' Dunbar ordered from the back seat. 'Bridge Street.'

'Reading Google Maps? There's hope for you yet.'

'Stop your yapping and concentrate.'

'Stern can't be that far ahead of us,' Harry said, as Evans swung the car round, siren blasting and blue lights flashing.

'Left at the bottom. And be careful, these are narrower roads. I like tractors but I don't want to be the mascot on the front of one.'

Evans slowed the car down then floored it when they

were on the road to the castle. A few minutes later they were getting closer. After the cemetery, it's second on the right,' Dunbar said.

When Evans found the road, it was even narrower. He had to slow down a bit. It was a one-lane road with white lines painted down the middle for a short distance, then a driver was on his own after that.

'I feel like I'm a rally driver,' Evans said, putting the headlights on and turning the siren and flashers off. He saw a straight piece of road and floored it again before slowing down.

They got down to the turnoff for the castle without meeting another car. Evans switched the headlights off before turning round by the houses where Stern had driven the Range Rover minutes earlier.

They came to the fork in the road where the castle keep could be seen, only now the sky was getting a bit darker, the sun finishing its duty for the day.

'Let us out here. Robbie, you come with me. Alex jump in, and take the car round to the keep there. We'll make our way through the gardens. We'll give you five minutes. If they take you by surprise, then they won't figure on us being here.'

They swapped seats and Alex drove off slowly, towards the castle, as Dunbar and Evans ran along the other road, hidden by the hedge.

'If Higgins is in there, he's not going to want to go back to prison,' Dunbar said. 'That makes him a very dangerous man.'

Evans looked at his boss. 'That makes two of us then.'

They entered the castle gardens.

FORTY-ONE

Alex pulled the police Vauxhall into the car park, lights off. There were trees here, obstructing their view of the keep, but it also meant they couldn't be seen from the tall building.

'The door's over there but there's also windows up above. They'll see us coming,' she said.

'Not if we stick close to that perimeter wall. The light's fading now and we've got dark clothing on.'

They got out of the car and stood by the trunk of a broad tree. The keep was tall and imposing, but on one side there was what looked like a house tacked onto it. This house held the entrance door. Another wall bordered the other side of the car park, and Harry assumed there was a drop into the gardens on the far side, as the road they had driven up was on an incline.

'Follow me,' he said, then he was off, hugging the stone wall. There were no lights on anywhere and they reached the walls of the keep, hugging the wall until they got to the entrance.

Higgins' Range Rover sat at the front door. He obviously hadn't been worried about being seen.

The door was unlocked. Harry quietly made his way in, closely followed by Alex. It was dark in here but their eyes started to adjust. They were in a stone-walled corridor of sorts. They followed it round to the right, then left, going round a corner, and saw another door facing them, which was open. Harry could see it led out into a courtyard, with the castle itself on the other side. Stone steps led up to their left and there was another doorway beyond them, wide open. Light was emitting from it and he could see a set of stone steps led down somewhere through the doorway.

He was about to move forward when the twin barrels of a shotgun touched his head.

'Welcome to the party,' Ralf St Charles said, stepping out of a hidden recess. 'Move. Through that door.'

He started pushing Harry with the gun when Alex grabbed it, but Ralf was too quick and pulled the barrels back. 'Get through that doorway,' he ordered. 'Down those steps and into that room. Your friends are waiting.'

Harry assumed he meant Dunbar and Evans and expected to see them there. Alex led the way and stepped through the door, looking at Candy Higgins cradling her daughter, and didn't see the log coming at her head. It connected, throwing her off her feet.

Harry saw her fall and turned as Higgins was bringing the log back for a strike at him. He sidestepped the clumsy swing and punched Higgins on the jaw, hooking him with a left on the nose. He grabbed the arm with the log and disarmed him before Ralf stepped into the room with the shotgun levelled.

Higgins staggered towards him, and Ralf smacked him with the gun and Higgins fell to the floor.

'Take that rope from over there and tie him to a chair,' he ordered. He was pointing the gun at Kenneth Conrad, who was sitting on the floor next to Candy. Harry hadn't recognised him at first.

Conrad got up and helped Higgins into the chair, rapidly tying him up.

There were two other chairs, but Candy was sitting on the floor, holding her daughter Christine, who looked terrified.

'Right, are there any more out there waiting to join the party?' Ralf said. He looked at Harry. 'Who knows we're here?'

'Nobody else. We came here because Higgins had written the address down on a piece of paper. We haven't called it in.'

He hoped Ralf didn't see though the bluff.

'Right. Now we're all here, let's begin.'

FORTY-TWO

Ralf St Charles didn't look like a maniac. Far from it. Harry had seen worse mental cases on the streets of Edinburgh, but what made him even more scary was the calmness about him. The shotgun was secondary.

Harry glanced across at Archie Higgins, sitting tied to the chair now, blood running down one side of his face. He was looking to see if the other man was still breathing.

'Why are you doing this?' he asked Ralf, but he knew damn well why the other man was doing this.

Ralf smiled and nodded across to Conrad. 'We were all friends, back in the day. Me, Benedict, Ken there, young Candy and Eddie. We all lived near Dunfermline, or in Candy's case, *in* Dunfermline. In the big house. We lived here, of course, in the even bigger house, but we didn't see ourselves as being above them. They were our friends.'

'Not your friends now, are they?' Harry said. His heart was racing a thousand beats a minute, it seemed, and he could feel his muscles tense. He held Alex, who was still unconscious.

Ralf smiled at Higgins. 'Poor Archie. He thought that his little girls were actually his. He found out at the hospital when they did blood work on Rebecca. They needed to do a transfusion, and they wanted to know her blood type. And since she was a blood donor, her mother knew her daughter's blood type. And when the doctors approached you with this, that's when it all went down the toilet.'

'You bastard. Your brother got what was coming to him. I saw to that. He died squealing like a pig, just like you're going to.'

Ralf smiled. 'Big words from a man who's tied up.'

Tears rolled down Candy's cheeks. She squeezed Christine harder, putting a hand round her head, as if that would stop her daughter from hearing. 'I'm sorry you had to find out this way, Archie.'

Higgins sneered at his wife. 'I trusted you.'

She looked him in the eyes. 'I'm sorry. I want to move on with my life. I want to start a new life with my daughter and her real father. That's why we got you here.'

'What are you talking about? Even if I go back to prison, you'll still be my fucking wife. You wouldn't dare leave me.'

'Listen to yourself. We're finished. You're going back to prison and I'm going to file for divorce. I've liquidated everything we owned because it was my money that started it all. You have nothing.'

'You bitch. I'll make sure you and your lover don't get far.'

She hesitated for a second.

'Why don't you let me tell him?' Higgins said.

Candy swung her head at him. 'You knew all this time?'

'Of course I did. It's why we're here now.'

'How?'

They all looked at Higgins. He took a deep breath and sighed. 'It was when Rebecca was lying in the hospital bed in a coma...'

FORTY-THREE

'Fuck this, it's been ten minutes,' Dunbar said. They were lying behind a large bush that could have been a small tree. He'd never had a green finger. As far as he was concerned, bushes were put on God's earth for dogs to pish on.

'Wait, boss, look.' Evans pointed to the stone steps that led to the back entrance to the castle. There were terraced lawns split by a stairway below the castle. Steps were on either side of the pathway nearest the detectives. A figure in black hugged the wall as he made his way to one of the sets of steps. He climbed the one on the right, and they saw him move quickly up the steps towards the castle, where once again, steps on either side of an arched wall led up to the courtyard.

It was almost full dark now, making the gardens in the grounds of the castle look ever more undesirable.

'Who the hell's that?' Evans said.

'How should I know? But why don't we go and introduce ourselves?'

'Tell me again why we're not waiting for armed response? And won't we get our arses kicked for going in there without a warrant?'

'Don't talk pish. First of all, armed response is God knows how long away, and if we see something suspicious, then that gives us the right to go in.'

'Go in where, though? The big mansion on the right, or the keep on the left?'

'I don't think whoever we're looking for is sitting have tea and scones in the big fucking hoose, Robbie. So get going, son. I don't want to lose that bastard, whoever he is.'

Evans took off like a cat, keeping low, and made his way up the steps like the figure had before them. Dunbar followed, at a slower pace.

At the top, he found Evans hiding behind a stone pillar. Much to Dunbar's chagrin, the younger detective wasn't even out of breath.

'Where have you been? My granny runs faster than that,' Evans said.

'Shut up. You're lucky I'm out of breath or I'd boot your arse.'

'I saw him go through a doorway over there,' Evans said. 'Let's go.'

'Give me a minute. I'm about to toss my fucking bag here.'

'You're not sweating, are you?' Evans asked.

'No, I thought I'd have a swim in the koi pond before

I came up here.' He bent over, his hands on his knees. 'If you ever suggest we go jogging up a set of steps again, I'll kill you with my bare hands.'

'He went inside. I want to go and see where he went.'

'Go then, Robbie. I'll catch up just after I go back down one flight and try and find the lung that fell oot halfway up.'

Evans took off, keeping low against the wall and ran as quietly as he could across the gravel car park. Dunbar watched as the orange lights on the side of the keep seemed to get brighter as the remainder of the daylight died an almost sudden death.

Then Evans was inside.

FORTY-FOUR

Archie Higgins had always hated hospitals. Like people all over the world, he loathed the smell. It was the smell he associated with his mother's death, so now, every time he set foot inside one, he saw his mother's pallid face as she lay dying in the bed with the crisp white sheets with the curtain pulled not quite all the way round.

The doctor approached them along the silent corridor. There were beeps and other noises but Higgins could only focus on the doctor, shutting everything else out.

'How's she doing, doc?'

'Stable, Mr Higgins. But we checked your blood type against Rebecca's and there's something we have to tell you.'

'No, please, doctor,' Candy said, standing up beside her husband and gripping his arm.

Higgins shrugged her off. 'Let him speak.'

The doctor paused for a second before looking Higgins in the eye. 'You have different blood types.'

'So.'

'I'm sorry. Mr Higgins, but in this instance, it means Rebecca isn't your biological daughter.'

Higgins didn't know what to say at first. 'What are you talking about?'

'Your blood type makes it impossible for you to be Rebecca's father. I'm sorry.'

As he walked away, Higgins turned towards Candy. 'Please tell me there's been some clerical mistake here, that my little girl is my little girl.'

The tears rolled down Candy's cheeks. 'I'm sorry, Archie. It was before we were married. We were just dating at the time.'

'We got married *because* you were pregnant. Fuck's sake.' He pushed her away as she tried to put her arm around him. 'Who's the father?'

'Benedict.'

'That snooty bastard? The one who attacked our fucking daughter!' He started shouting and pointing along the corridor to the room where their daughter lay dying. 'You have got to be fucking kidding me!'

'I'm sorry. I've known him longer than I've known you.'

'And that makes it alright, does it?'

'It was a one-off.'

Higgins' security chief, Eddie Wise was standing along the other end of the corridor. 'Eddie! Here, now.'

Eddie strode towards them. Higgins started issuing orders before he'd even reached them.

'You're coming with me. We have to go and talk to somebody. Let's go.' He started walking away, but then stopped and turned to his wife. 'We'll talk about this later.'

FORTY-FIVE

Harry felt his anger rising. He thought Alex's breathing was getting shallower. 'Listen, Ralf, my sergeant needs a doctor. She's badly injured and I don't think she's going to make it.'

'In a minute, I promise.'

'Let me look at her,' Kenneth Conrad said, coming closer. Harry moved slightly, not wanting him to touch her.

'I'm a doctor, remember?' He ignored the shotgun tracking him and knelt down. He put his hands on her neck for a second, then opened each of her eyes.

'How's she looking?'

'More than likely a concussion. Just sit with her head a little bit higher, more forward just to straighten out her airway. Her pulse is steady. I would say she's going to be just fine.'

'Thanks.'

Conrad nodded and went back over to Candy and Christine.

'You were telling us about going to see Benedict St Charles,' Harry said, holding Alex closer to him.

Higgins looked at him. 'We got to the flat St Charles had, and I told Eddie Wise to kill the bastard. I'd told him that St Charles was the father of my daughter. Eddie didn't believe it. When we confronted the snobby bastard, he was all but pishing himself.' Higgins grinned. 'I told him I knew about what he had done. He was babbling on about not being their father, that I was wrong. He hadn't attacked Rebecca either. He said he and that twat there were going to another dance at the hotel, and they just happened to be passing the room when they saw Christine screaming and Becca lying on the floor.'

He paused for breath. 'I had a feeling St Charles wasn't the father, that Candy had been spinning me a line. Eddie hesitated again, so I took out my knife and I stabbed St Charles to death. Then you know the rest. Except one thing; I suspected that Candy had been with somebody else. You, Conrad. You were seen with my wife, but I didn't even know who you were.'

'How did you find out?' Conrad looked unflinchingly at Higgins.

'Money, that's how. When you have it, you can pay for the best investigators. Oh, you have to believe I wanted my men to rip you apart, but that would have been too easy. I wanted to know everything there was to know about you. And what did I find out? You met my Candy long before I did. The team of investigators talked to a lot of people, and they made the connection. They even guessed where the tryst might have happened, going by the timeframe of nine months before Rebecca was born.'

Conrad made a face. 'Let me hear it then.'

'You were in the Territorial Army, twenty years ago. In the 205 Scottish Field Hospital. Back then, there were four units, one of which was in Glasgow. They trained some weekends with the other units, up at the Cultybraggan Camp, not far from Crieff. Which isn't a stone's throw from the hunting lodge that Candy's dad owned, near the loch.' He looked at Conrad and grinned but his face was full of menace. 'How am I doing so far?'

'I'm impressed. Your team did some good work. We did indeed meet when I was at the camp. I hadn't seen Candy for years. She was staying at the hunting lodge and I had a free pass for the night, so we went there and one thing led to another. I wanted to marry her, but she was going with you, and she said she didn't want to hurt you.'

'Good for her. But that wasn't all my investigators found out; young Eddie Wise was also a foster child at that woman's house. And he grew up with you two. Good old Eddie. That's why I wanted Hugh to shoot him, but my wife said she wanted to. She let him escape.'

'Can you blame me? He wasn't to blame for Rebecca's death,' Candy said.

'What would you have done if Hugh had insisted?' Conrad asked.

Candy grinned. 'I put two training slugs in the shotgun. He would have been able to run even if that gorilla had pointed the gun at him.'

'Loyalty to the end,' Higgins said and spat on the stone floor.

'There's one thing that's puzzling me,' Harry said to Higgins.

'What's that?'

'How come you didn't have Conrad topped in prison?'

'That would have been too easy. No, I wanted to get him somewhere quiet and take care of him myself. A few notes sent to somebody I know in the Crown Office, and suddenly Conrad was going to court the same day I was. It was a gamble, whether he would escape with me or not, but he had already told me that he was innocent. Well, don't they all? But I knew that he was because I was the one who had set him up. I thought he'd want to get out and try and prove his innocence. On the way to court, I told him he would have a chance to prove himself, but I didn't go into details. When we were leaving, I gave him money, a phone and a number to call. He didn't call me. I didn't figure he would call this twat instead.'

Harry nodded his head. 'You were controlling him. Getting him to come to you so you could deal with him. And you had Hugh Stern kill Conrad's foster mother, just to make sure we would step up our hunt for him.'

'Very clever, McNeil. You would have found him dead, case closed.'

'Except it went a little awry. But let me ask you; what was going to become of Candy and Christine?'

'Candy would have gone off with Conrad, if you see what I mean. That's what they had planned. My plan was, if Candy didn't want to come with me to South America, they would have ended up in the ground.'

'Enough!' Ralf shouted. 'I don't care what you all would have done. Higgins killed my brother and now he's going to pay. He's going back to prison.'

'Go on, keep denying it,' Higgins said. 'Your brother killed my daughter.'

'He did not kill your daughter!' Ralf's voice screamed in the stone room, reverberating off the walls.

'Yes he fucking did!' Higgins shouted back, equally loud.

'No, he didn't, I did!'

They all fell silent and looked at Christine, who had pushed away from her mother.

'What did you say?' Candy said to her. Christine looked at her, then Higgins.

'I said, it was me who killed Rebecca. It was an accident, honest.'

'What do you mean you killed her?' Higgins said, his voice dry now. Christine, who hadn't uttered a word in two years, now couldn't hold back the words.

'We argued. She said that you weren't her dad. I told her to shut up but she kept going on and on, saying that you weren't my dad either. I tried to hit her but she jumped onto the bed. I pushed her and she fell, landing on the bedside cabinet and she hit her head on the floor. I screamed and two men rushed in. The door was open and they saw Rebecca lying there. They tried to help but then everybody came running in and they left. But that man was right; his brother didn't kill Rebecca. I did. It was an accident.'

Higgins was stunned into silence. Candy started crying and looked at her daughter.

'Tell me the truth, Mum,' the young girl said. 'Is he my dad?' She nodded towards Higgins who was still trying to undo the ropes that were binding him to the chair.

Candy looked into her daughter's eyes before answering. 'No.' Her voice was a whisper.

'Then who is?'

Candy looked at Conrad. 'He is. Your sister was right. I'm sorry.' Then she looked at Higgins. 'I couldn't tell you, obviously.'

'Don't even fucking look at me.'

Candy looked away, and Harry could see in her face that she was glad her husband was tied up.

Harry looked at Higgins. 'This was all for nothing. You killed Benedict St Charles because you thought he'd killed Rebecca. Then you found out Kenneth Conrad there was the real father of your children, so you got him out with you, so you could kill him. You set him up, making it look like he had killed his patients.'

Then they saw a hand wrap itself round Ralf's face and a figure grabbed the shotgun from him. Ralf turned round and was rewarded with the butt of the gun rammed into his face.

'He's lying about killing Benedict St Charles. I killed him,' Hugh Stern said, but Conrad looked aghast.

He was looking at the face of Michael Salamin.

FORTY-SIX

'You took your bloody time,' Archie Higgins said. 'Untie me.'

Stern looked at him like he was about to say something but then he brought a knife out of his pocket and cut the ropes, still holding onto the shotgun.

'Christ, my wrists are killing me.' He rubbed them before turning to Stern. 'Give me the gun.'

Stern handed it over. Higgins grinned. 'Bet you're not too confident now, eh, Conrad?' Higgins levelled the gun at the doctor but then his eyes went wide and he stood staring at the wall. Stern was standing close behind him, and then they all saw the movement as he pulled the knife out of Higgins' back and plunged it in again.

Higgins was still standing, being supported by Stern who had plunged the knife all the way into Higgins' heart. Blood started running out of Higgins' mouth as Stern pulled the knife out and reached round for the shotgun before pushing Higgins to the floor, where he lay still, the patch of blood on his back spreading. He put the knife away after wiping it on Higgins' shirt.

'I just severed my ties with Higgins,' Stern said. 'Despite what I did to frame you, Conrad, I actually liked you. I couldn't let Higgins destroy what you have with his wife. He deserved what he got.'

Candy looked shocked, her face pale. She held her daughter's face against her, shielding her from the scene playing out before their eyes. 'You could have killed Eddie that night. Why didn't you?'

Stern smiled. 'Your husband was paying me to set up Conrad there. I don't do freebies for anybody. I kill for my own pleasure. Your husband was the only one who paid me, but I wasn't going to just kill willy-nilly. Eddie did nothing to me so I couldn't care less if he made off.'

'Higgins paid you to frame Conrad?' Harry said, still holding on tight to Alex.

'Yes. I killed four of his patients.'

'We thought he had killed over a hundred,' Harry said.

'A hundred? No, that was all mind games. The press wasn't hungry for a doctor who had killed four patients, but they lapped it up when they thought it was over a hundred. Just give them some small snippet of information, or should I say, *mis*information, and they'll run with it. That's what we did, and the next thing you know, Conrad's being treated like Jack the Ripper.'

'So what now? You kill Ralf and disappear?' Harry said. 'Ride away into the sunset?'

Stern pointed the shotgun towards Harry but he didn't flinch. He was concentrating on holding Alex.

'That's the way it goes. I'm finished with this doctor lark. I'd rather take lives than save them. More fun that way.'

'What are you going to do with us, Hugh?' Candy asked.

'I've been thinking about that. Thus far, I've been helping Higgins, but now that we've parted company, I'll be going solo. But then I'll have left witnesses.'

'There's six of us here,' Harry said, 'not including Higgins, who is in no way able to help. What are you going to do? If you shoot two of us, we can be all over you before you reload.'

Stern laughed out loud. 'One man, who I'm sure has a broken nose and looks stunned,' he said, nodding to the prone figure of Ralf St Charles. 'One woman, a young girl, who looks like she couldn't fight her way through a paper hanky. One female who's unconscious. That just leaves you and Conrad. One each. I only need two rounds. Then I can take my time reloading.'

'Assuming Ralf has more rounds in his pockets,' Harry said.

'If he hasn't, then there's always my knife.'

He levelled the gun at Harry and watched as the detective covered Alex's body with his own, shielding her. Small comfort but if he was going to die, he wanted her to live, if possible.

'Isn't that nice?' Stern said, just as he felt his hair being grabbed and a hand grabbing the shotgun, which fired, the sound deafening in the small room. The buck-shot chipped the stone ceiling then the gun went off again.

Harry tried to jump up as he saw Robbie Evans grappling with the big man. Stern grabbed the shotgun in both hands, pushed Evans against Dunbar, and they both fell.

He turned and fled out of the door.

'Get the women!' Harry shouted.

Then they saw the first tendrils of smoke.

FORTY-SEVEN

'Harry, watch!' Jimmy Dunbar shouted, as he struggled to sit up. 'He's poured petrol on the doorway up those stairs.'

As Harry looked round, a wall of flame danced outside the room they were in. He was struggling against the ropes that bound his hands and feet. He pulled at the rope at his ankles and managed to get it off but the room was filling with smoke.

Conrad helped Candy to her feet and got hold of Christine. They made it to the door but the flames were intensifying. They couldn't get out.

Harry got to his feet but the room swam. The blood that had run down his face had dried and he blinked, trying to get his bearings. Tried to get the room to stop spinning.

Dunbar got to his feet and tried to look out into the corridor beyond, but he couldn't see through the flames licking at the wood.

'Jesus, we're trapped.'

'No, we're not.' A voice from the floor. Ralf St Charles.

'Can't you see the fire?' Dunbar shouted at him.

'Haven't you ever heard of a priest hole? We have one over here.' He got to his feet, blood still running from his nose where Stern had hit him. He staggered to the log fireplace and reached up inside. He grabbed hold of a metal rod with a handle and pulled hard. The back of the fireplace swung inwards.

'Right along to the end. There's a flight of stairs. There's a wooden handle. It turns a door in the walk-in pantry in the kitchen that's used for selling ice cream to tourists. It's on the other side of the keep.'

Dunbar looked at him. 'This was your Plan B?'

'Of course. You know what Higgins is like.'

Evans rushed over to Harry who was struggling to drag Alex. 'I've got her, sir. Just go with Jimmy.'

Harry was reluctant, but Dunbar helped him, following Conrad and Candy along with Christine.

Evans had Alex under the arms and was dragging her. Ralf took out his phone and put the flashlight on. It was difficult to see but not impossible. He pushed the door in the fireplace closed. He brought up the rear and watched as Conrad found the wooden handle and turned it. It was just like a door opening and suddenly they were in a kitchen.

Evans laid Alex down gently on the cold, tiled floor.

'We're safe,' Harry said.

'I don't think we're ever going to be safe while that bastard is still on the loose,' Dunbar said.

FORTY-EIGHT

Hugh Stern ran up the stairs and made his way across the entrance area, smiling to himself. Pouring the petrol before he went in was one of his better ideas. He'd seen the machinery before he entered and found the can of petrol. They could all burn to death and he'd be away before the fire brigade could identify the bodies. They'd all be burnt like barbeque sausages.

It was full dark now but the outside was slightly lighter than in here. The door was still open leading to the courtyard. He was approaching it when a figure stepped into view.

'Well, well, if it isn't good old Hugh, the granny killer.' Eddie Wise stood and smiled at him.

'God, they always say the bad penny rolls back into town. And here you are. If you want them, they're down-stairs burning to a crisp.' Stern laughed as he walked towards Eddie, then he brought his knife from behind his back and lunged.

Eddie easily sidestepped the thrusting blade and grabbed Stern's arm, twisting hard. But Stern wasn't a pushover. He moved round, counteracting the twist and lashed out with his other hand, the back of his fist connecting with Wise's face.

Eddie was stunned for a second which gave Stern time to pull free. Stern lashed out with the knife and caught Eddie in the side.

Eddie gasped and fell sideways. Stern leaned down. 'If I ever see you again, Eddie, I'll put this through your heart.'

Stern walked away, out into the night, turning to cut across the courtyard where he'd left his car.

Somebody was sitting on the bonnet.

'Aw, come on,' he said out loud. His boots crunched on the gravel. The white lights on the wall of the keep shone down onto the car, illuminating Harry McNeil.

'Hugh Stern, you're under arrest,' Harry said, standing up. His head still hurt like hell and he wasn't sure he was going to be able to stand for much longer. Sirens could be heard a distance away.

'Hear that?' Stern said. 'That's the ambulance coming to take you away on a stretcher.'

'Really now?' Robbie Evans said, stepping out from behind a Volvo SUV. 'I would say that's it coming for you, Stern. Or you can wait for a patrol car. Your choice.'

Stern laughed. 'Och, it wouldn't be right hitting a wee laddie.'

They all heard the scuff of shoes on the gravel behind Stern. He turned to look and saw Jimmy

Dunbar. 'I think that wee laddie might want to give it a go.'

Evans took his jacket off and pulled his belt out of the loops in his trousers.

Stern made a face. 'I'm going to fucking gut you all like fish. You first.' He started speed walking towards Evans, his eyes laser focused. When he got closer he let out a tremendous yell, like he was going into battle.

Then he fell onto the gravel and started twitching. Harry held the Taser in his right hand as Dunbar came running up behind the big man and kicked him hard between the legs.

'I had it covered, Jimmy,' Harry said, his finger still on the Taser.

'Did you fuck. You're almost on your arse. Let him go now,' Dunbar said and slapped the cuffs onto Stern's wrists that were now behind his back.

'Now that's what I call team work,' Evans said. 'I told you he'd want to have a go at me.'

'Never mind that, just get your bloody belt back on before you start flashing your skids.'

'Bastards,' Stern said, then Harry gave him another little jolt.

A couple of minutes later, a fleet of patrol cars came screaming into the courtyard, followed by a couple of ambulances.

'Get this piece of shit into the back of a car,' Harry said to the first couple of uniforms just as the first fire engine appeared. Evans directed them to where the fire was.

'You're looking pale there, Harry,' Dunbar said.

'I'll be fine. We have more important things to worry about. Like Ralf St Charles.'

'We're going to have to take them all in, get everything on paper. But if Candy came here willingly to try and trap her husband, then Ralf hasn't done anything illegal.'

'Nor Conrad. We heard Stern's confession.'

'Christ, the PF is going to have some details to work out, what with young Christine saying she accidentally killed her sister.'

A uniform approached. 'There's a man lying in the doorway at the entrance, bleeding like he's been stabbed.'

'Who the hell's that?' Dunbar said.

They walked over as a medic was attending him. Firemen had dragged him away from the fire.

'Eddie Wise, as I live and breathe,' Dunbar said. He turned to Harry. 'One of Higgins' men.'

'I tried to stop Stern,' Eddie said, 'but he got away.'

'Don't worry, we got him,' Harry said, still feeling light-headed.

'We're going to have to have a wee chat after you get patched up,' Dunbar said.

'I'll tell you everything I know. That bastard killed my friends in the fire down there.'

They looked at the flames licking inside the hallway, being brought under control by the firefighters.

'We were down there, too. We got out a back way. Conrad and Candy are safe,' Dunbar said.

'What about Higgins?'

Harry shook his head. 'He didn't make it.' Then he felt the world spin but Evans put a hand on his arm. The feeling passed. He nodded at the younger detective who let him go.

'I want to go and see Alex,' Harry said.

'I'll come with you,' Evans said.

'Thanks for getting her out of there,' Harry said. 'I couldn't have done it. I would have stayed with her and we both would have died.'

'I'm sure you would have found the strength, sir. In fact, I recall you helping me get her through that fireplace.'

'That was just supporting her legs for a minute. You did all the hard work.'

'Put a positive spin on it; you helped me get her out of that room and when she was safe, you made sure everybody else got out.'

'I like the sound of that.' They reached the back of the ambulance just as they were securing the stretcher that Alex was on.

'I'll go with her.' He turned to look at Evans. 'You'll go a long way, son.'

Then the ambulance door was closed.

FORTY-NINE

The Western General hospital in Edinburgh was buzzing by the time Harry got to Alex's ward. She was in bed with a bandage round her head.

'How are you feeling?' he asked her. He was already dressed, having been visited by the doctor and given the all clear.

'Better now that I see you have a wee shaved patch on your head. And stitches too? Most men would have just bought a girl a bunch of flowers, but you went the extra mile and got into a fight with a psycho.'

'I aim to please.' He sat down on the edge of her bed. 'But you didn't answer my question.'

'I'm fine. Just a headache now.'

Harry knew she was making light of it, but the doctor had told him it could have been a lot more serious. If Higgins had hit her head any harder, there could have been a lot more damage. Conrad had been right in his diagnosis; a slight concussion from which she would recover, with plenty of rest for the next two weeks.

'I was worried about you.' He reached out and held her hand. 'Listen, I had this all planned out, but considering life can change in a heartbeat, I wanted to ask you this now. It's not very romantic, I know, but you know I love you and want to spend the rest of my life with you. So, with that in mind, will you marry me?'

She laughed. 'Of course I will. I love you, Harry McNeil. And just wait 'til we tell our grandchildren how you proposed.'

He leaned over and kissed her just as the door opened wider.

'Aye, aye. What an animal. He can't leave that lassie alone for a minute, even when she's in a hospital bed,' Jimmy Dunbar said as he and Robbie Evans came in.

'Never heard of knocking?' Harry said.

'The door was practically wide open, son. That was an invitation for us to enter.'

'Storm in, more like.' He grinned and got up off the bed.

'Harry just asked me to marry him,' Alex said. 'And before you come out with some smart-arsed remark, no, the bump on his head isn't affecting him.'

'We wouldn't suggest anything of the sort,' Evans said, grinning. He looked at Harry. 'You do know where you are, don't you, sir?'

'Shut up, Robbie,' Dunbar said. 'Leave the lassie to bask in her happiness.'

'Grab a seat,' Harry said, sitting back down on the bed.

The Glasgow detectives both sat on chairs. 'We've been in a meeting with the senior officers and Norma Banks, the PF, all morning.'

'About time you met Norma Banks,' Harry said.

'She's a pit bull, let me tell you. But on our side and she's pleased we managed to locate Archie Higgins, even if it meant he went back in a body bag. She'll be talking to her Strathclyde counterpart this afternoon.'

'Did she mention what charges are going to be brought?' Alex said.

'As we talked about, Ralf St Charles made it look like both Candy and Christine were abducted, but they weren't, that was just a ploy. They wanted Higgins captured, so Candy could leave with Conrad. They knew he was innocent. No charges are being brought against any of them. Eddie Wise? They're going to look into him, but if they can't find anything rock solid, I don't think they'll bring anything against him. Conrad will be given prison time for escaping, but Banks said it will probably be time served, so he won't see prison again. The charges of murder against him will be dropped and his name publicly cleared.'

'They're going to throw the book at Hugh Stern though. He's already claiming police brutality,' Evans said. 'Considering he murdered old women, I don't think that's going to stick.'

Harry looked at Dunbar before speaking. 'What about young Christine? She admitted to killing her sister.'

Dunbar shook his head. 'The lassie's spent two years in a care home. I don't think they're going to press charges. They have bigger fish to fry.'

'Good. If Conrad and Candy take her away from all of this, they can start a new life.'

'When I spoke to Candy, she said they're going to stay in the hunting lodge. Live in the country well away from Glasgow.'

'I think that's a good idea. But what about Higgins' little kingdom?' Alex asked.

'What kingdom, Alex? Candy sold off most of his businesses, but it was her family's money that bankrolled them to begin with, and nothing was in his name, so everything belonged to her by default. She was counting on him getting life in prison so she could live in peace.'

'There's nothing standing in her way, so she should be fine.'

They chit-chatted for a little while before Dunbar and Evans stood up. 'Time for us to head back west.'

'He's missing Scooby,' Evans said.

'Belt up, sergeant. Talking of which, I never want to see a display like that again.'

'Like what?'

'Taking your belt off. If your troosers had landed round your ankles, you would have scarred us for life.'

'It seems I missed all the fun when I was in the back of the ambulance,' Alex said, grinning.

'He's only jealous,' Evans said.

'Don't worry, Alex, you didn't miss much. That's why his girlfriend dumped him.'

Evans shook his head. 'It was a mutual parting of the ways.'

'Was it now? I'll bet. But we better part ways with our friends here. Take care of yourself, or rather, have him take care of you,' Dunbar said, leaning over to kiss her on the cheek. 'Remember to have Chance give me a call.'

Evans did the same and then they left the ward, closing the door behind them.

'I can't wait to get back home,' Alex said. 'I'll have to call my mum to tell her about us getting engaged.'

'Just don't get too excited. You have to rest.'

'You mean, you haven't bought the ring yet.' She grinned at him.

'The ring for what?'

'You know.'

'What? I've had a bump on the heid, remember?'

'Harry McNeil, I swear to God...'

'I already have it at home. I was just biding my time.'

'You get there in the end, that's the main thing.'

'Story of my life,' Harry said. 'Just so you know what you're letting yourself in for.'

'Way ahead of you there, lover boy. Way ahead of you.'

AFTERWORD

First of all, I just want to say, I have never been in court, so the inside of the High Court in Edinburgh is a mystery to me. I used literary license for this story. I also don't know much about the transport of prisoners, but did some research online, and made a lot of the stuff up. However, Securicor Omega Express *did* have a parcel depot at South Gyle.

Thank you to my advanced reader team, and welcome aboard some new members, Liz Phillips, Michelle Cooper, Kara Page, Rachel Jones and Mike Hughes.

A huge thank you to all my readers who continue to read Harry McNeil and his exploits. Especially to Sylvia Fox Lanspery.

And of course, to my wife and daughters for their support.

If I could ask you to please leave a review for this

book, that would be terrific. I do appreciate every honest opinion.

Stay safe my friends.

John Carson
    May 2020
    New York

ABOUT THE AUTHOR

John Carson is originally from Edinburgh, Scotland, but now lives in New York State with his wife and family. And two dogs. And four cats.

website - johncarsonauthor.com
Facebook - JohnCarsonAuthor
Twitter - JohnCarsonBooks
Instagram - JohnCarsonAuthor

Printed in Great Britain
by Amazon

22132264R00148